PRAISE FOR *STARS IN HIS EYES*

"Drawing on material of exceptional dramatic richness, Martí Gironell has written a story of personal success starring a man who pursued a dream and didn't stop until he turned it into a reality."

—*El 3 de Vuit*

"A great story."

—*El Punt Avui*

"Gironell manages to reveal the most vulnerable side of his character, as with Gatsby, the inner solitude of the successful."

—*La Vanguardia*

"A fictionalized story of a truly filmic life."

—*Segre Lectura*

"A novel that will surely be a sales success and may even end up on-screen."

—*El Diario Montañés*

"Martí Gironell has turned a life full of adventure into a novel."

—*La Razón*

"A cinematic life in the heart of the dream factory . . . A fascinating and inimitable character."

—*Diario de León*

Stars in His Eyes

Stars in His Eyes

MARTÍ GIRONELL

Translated by Adrian Nathan West

amazoncrossing

Previously published as *La força d'un destí* by Columna Edicions in Spain in 2018. Translated from Catalan by Adrian Nathan West. First published in English by AmazonCrossing in 2019.

Published by AmazonCrossing, Seattle

www.apub.com

Amazon, the Amazon logo, and AmazonCrossing are trademarks of Amazon.com, Inc., or its affiliates.

ISBN-13: 9781542040624 (hardcover)
ISBN-10: 1542040620 (hardcover)
ISBN-13: 9781542040631 (paperback)
ISBN-10: 1542040639 (paperback)

Cover design by Faceout Studio, Derek Thornton

Title treatment by Kimberly Glyder

Printed in the United States of America

First edition

For my wife, Eva, and my children, Quim and Pep.
For my parents, Carme and Martí.

Do what you can, with what you have, where you are.

—Squire Bill Widener, as quoted by Theodore Roosevelt

CHAPTER 1

Growl you may, but go you must!

The words were tattooed on the forearm of the husky black man with the broad back, who was looking down at the small, pale, trembling boy.

"But go you must?" Ceferino Carrión mumbled nervously in halting English.

Completing the tattoo were a sailboat surrounded by thick rope, an eagle with outstretched wings, and an anchor. The man who'd cornered him, clearly a crew member of the enormous ship Ceferino had crept onto as a stowaway, threw his head back in laughter.

"Will you tell?" Ceferino asked, this time in slightly less broken French.

"Don't worry, I mean you no harm," the sailor responded, showing off a row of very white teeth. The boy was still panting and had to struggle to meet the sailor's eyes. "You thirsty? Hungry, maybe?"

The man crouched down beside him and took a chocolate bar from his pocket. Cefe, who had no idea how many hours he'd been hidden on the ship, snatched it from the man's hands and swallowed it down quickly, barely bothering to unwrap it. His eyes, already begging silently for a second helping, came to rest on the letters embroidered on the front of the man's hat, a white brimless cap bearing the word *Liberté*.

Liberty! Pray God it's a sign, Cefe thought, though he knew better than to lower his guard. He had already failed seven times to make it onto a ship. For weeks upon weeks, he'd tramped around the port at Le Havre with his companions, Pedro and Jaime, their eyes peeled for a shot at slipping onto one of those immense vessels and making their way toward New York. The Promised Land, they called it. The land of *liberté.*

For Ceferino and his friends, the two years since they'd left Barcelona had been one long, grueling pilgrimage. They had all come of age in that time, but not one had any intention of waiting for their draft papers to come in, forcing them to complete their service in the fascist army. *I'll never serve the side that killed my people,* Cefe told himself over and over when his spirits lagged.

The boys were also running from the lack of opportunity in the gray, dark, early years of Franco's dictatorship in Spain. They had crossed the Pyrenees on foot until they reached Bayonne, then had followed the Atlantic coast of France under the harshest conditions. They took any job they could find to put food in their mouths and a roof over their heads. They'd passed through Bordeaux during the weeks of the grape harvest; their time there stretched on through twelve-hour days of unceasing work. The boys walked among the vine rows on the banks of the Garonne, at the feet of the famous and grandiose châteaux, which Ceferino would contemplate in silence while he learned to distinguish the different varieties of grapes they were picking.

The only time they let themselves linger for a spell was in Paris. Ceferino had worked as a waiter and cook in the popular nightspots, learning the language and developing a taste for jazz. But soon, the news came that he'd been declared a fugitive in his home country. He was no longer safe. It was time, he decided, to rebel, to put an ocean between himself and his problems. He set his eyes doggedly on a North America that had once been the stuff of legend, a magical place that felt closer, more real with every second.

And now, at twenty-one, when his most longed-for dream was almost within his grasp, a brawny seaman was standing in his way. It wouldn't be long before the ship started its motors. The man still had time to alert the authorities, drag the boy back to terra firma—the best-case scenario—and save himself a whole load of problems. Never before had Cefe missed his brothers in misfortune as much as he did just then. He knew his decision to strike out on his own had put him in a vulnerable situation. He was traveling alone, with nothing but the clothes on his back—a blue shirt, beige pants, and a worn-out pair of lace-ups. Those and a sheaf of documents to remind him where he came from, where he was going, and who he was leaving behind.

"What's your name?" the sailor asked him gently.

"Ceferino," he replied, before adding, "Cefe."

"Everyone calls me Joe. You coming from Spain?"

He said that he was.

"You're not the first kid to try and make it across the Atlantic. A lot of hopes and dreams and not much in the way of possessions to make it through a real long journey," the sailor said, using slightly broken Spanish in an attempt to calm the boy down. "I don't suppose you have any money, or food, or clothes? Might as well tell you, the place you've picked to hole up isn't well suited to the cold Atlantic nights."

The boy shook his head to each of the sailor's conjectures, looking balefully around at the damp, windswept corner he had chosen to hide in.

"What will you do with me?" Ceferino gathered the courage to ask.

"I already told you, you got nothing to worry about."

"Why should I believe you?"

"I know how to keep a secret. That's what makes a person strong. Can I trust you with one?"

The question caught the boy by surprise.

"Being a sailor's not my only job on this ship. And this, uh . . . other job, let's say, the captain don't know nothing about it," the sailor said conspiratorially.

Perhaps, Ceferino thought, this was the moment when his integrity would be put to the test. He knew more than a few grim stories with dark finales out on the open sea.

"A group of us sailors who make the regular route from Le Havre to New York, we put together a little venture bringing over people like yourself," he said, pointing at the kid. "Making sure they get across safely. But it ain't easy—there's a lot more sailors against helping out stowaways than there are willing to do it. So if you want to make it, we'll have to be very careful."

The kid nodded mechanically, unsure whether he could trust this man.

"Don't you worry. I'll take care of you," the sailor assured him. "If the currents are good to us and we don't come across any obstacles, we'll be docking in New York in eight days." Joe smiled and patted the boy gently on the shoulder.

For the first time during the conversation, Ceferino couldn't suppress his smile. His thoughts had jumped ahead in time, and he imagined himself grazing the peaks of the city's skyscrapers with his fingertips. Then the noise of the onboard sirens brought him back to reality.

"We're about to haul anchor, and I need to get to my post. Don't you come out of your hiding place. Later I'll come see how you are. I'll bring you water, a bite to eat, and a blanket later on."

The sailor gave him his hand to shake, in this way sealing their pact of brotherhood, then vanished into the darkness of the ship's hold. Ceferino felt an emptiness, in the pit of his stomach and beyond. Suddenly, his nerves, his anguish, and all the frustration and tension he'd accumulated those past few months came unmoored and crashed against him. He broke into tears. It was like a storm in autumn—intense but mercifully brief. Calm followed in time, and his breathing slowed to match the sedate movements of the ship being dragged out by the tugboats. His journey, which had begun so long ago, would soon cover its first nautical mile. But Ceferino knew nothing of that. He had fallen asleep.

The prediction of eight days' travel was optimistic. The voyage would last two long weeks.

First he had to get used to the shadows, which were something less than utter darkness, and to the silence, which wasn't quite silence, either. Above all, he had to get used to the isolation, the constant tension, the danger of being found by some crew member less sensitive to his plight than his protector had been. *Everyone calls me Joe.* Cefe was unable to hide his gratitude for the big man's visits and companionship, and it seemed the feeling was mutual.

This was far and away the longest trip he'd ever taken in his life, yet all he could do was sit still, quiet, closed up in a cramped space no larger than a jail cell. It was impossible not to fill that period of solitude and waiting with memories. Inevitably, with so much time to wrestle with his thoughts, those thoughts would turn to his father.

Ceferino had only gotten to visit his father in prison one time, but that was enough never to forget it. The Carrións were a family that believed in the values of the Republic and knew what it meant to defend its ideals. One day, his father didn't come home. In the last days of the Civil War, they had fingered him as a political commissar for the Reds. Ceferino didn't see him until two months later.

"Did you bring me some cigarettes?" Antonio Carrión had said, winking at his son.

His father was in bad shape, but he still held his head high, showing the same serenity, laced with an iron will, as always. Ceferino tried to convince himself the guards' treatment of his father wasn't as bad as he'd heard, that his captors had been able to see what a good person his father was. He wasn't naive, but he loved his father so much and that was the only possibility he could accept without going mad, even after he saw the painful emptiness behind the man's tired eyes.

"Don't worry, boy. Even if they pull out my teeth, I won't pledge allegiance to this godforsaken regime that's trying to wipe us out."

"If you say that, they'll never let you go. And you didn't do anything wrong," the child pleaded, his eyes fixed on his father's sad smile.

"What's the point of being free if you can't think or act according to your beliefs?" His father's voice was so firm and touched him so deeply that Ceferino's sorrow only grew. "No one should be able to control another person's life or bend their will. You listen to me, boy: *you* make your choices. You and you alone."

Many months later, Ceferino's father returned home. He never talked about his time in prison, and he never showed any bitterness. He wanted his life back, and since he wasn't the type of man to sit idle for long, when the opportunity came to enlist in the merchant marine with his older son, he didn't let it slip by. Months later, both lost their lives in an incident the regime's official sources covered up with customary diligence.

That was eight years ago already. July 1, 1941. Also in summertime, on the open sea.

"What happened to them?" the sailor asked.

"From what we were told, the ship was on a route that docked at a German port, carrying clandestine war materials for the Third Reich. The British fleet smelled something funny and sank it."

The sailor looked at the boy with compassion. He drew a metal flask from his pocket and shared it with Ceferino.

"We all lost someone we loved in the war," he said.

They drank in silence until the alarm announcing the changing of the guard on deck separated them.

Ever since the day of his father's and brother's deaths—though he kept it to himself, thinking that to say it aloud would be to dishonor their memory—Ceferino had felt an insuperable revulsion toward the sea, a kind of visceral dislike that gnawed at him from inside.

The national newspapers didn't publish a single line about the sinking of the merchant vessel from the Carandini shipping firm. The family viewed their silence as a way for Franco's regime to keep up the facade of neutrality during the goddamn war. That silence, of course, kept them from being able to seek any sort of compensation. Ceferino's mother had to move heaven and earth to get her widow's pension; she was lucky to have the parish priest on her side. The one gesture of humanity came from Enasa, the national truck company, or rather its founder, Wilfredo Ricart. Enasa manufactured heavy vehicles—vans, trucks, and cars—responding to a vital need of the state after the devastation of the Civil War. Located in the Barcelona neighborhood of La Sagrera and founded at the behest of the National Institute of Industry, Ricart's company gave jobs to all the children, brothers, and other immediate family of the victims of the incident. The owner was a seaman's son; he was moved by the tragedy, and he wanted to do something to help. And that was how, cursing and gritting his teeth—because there was no way around it, he was serving Franco's cause—Ceferino became a sheet-metal worker, a model employee, despite everything. During break time, he shared conversation and cigarettes with two young men who'd been scarred by the regime, who were as unhappy as he was, and who planned to flee the country.

"The clock's ticking for me to turn nineteen. After that, they'll call me up," Ceferino said to them with indignation, which he underlined by throwing his cigarette to the ground and crushing it beneath his shoe. "And I'm not about to give up my best days for a goddamn country that killed my father and my brother." The others nodded in silent assent.

In the hold of the ship, as the days passed, Cefe longed for these lost friends. Once, the sailor asked him what methods they used to try and sneak aboard the other vessels. Joe admired how they hadn't given up after the third or fourth attempt. Ceferino made a list for him. They had tried everything you could think of: hiding among grain sacks, breaking into a shipping container and creeping in, even hiding in a car just before it was loaded on board with a crane. His expression turned glum when he recalled the two times they had truly feared for their safety, after unsympathetic crew members had discovered them: "The first time," Ceferino explained, "they found us huddled in a lifeboat, on the port side; the second, they surprised us in the ship's hold when the guards were making their rounds."

The episode that had left the deepest mark on his friends took place on their seventh and final try. Frustration had started to wear at the young men's spirits, and they were thinking of giving up and making a go of it in France. But then they met a sailor who offered, between glasses of wine and shots of rum, to get them on a ship moored in the port in exchange for what money they'd managed to scrape together. Once there, they were locked in a small cabin—for reasons of safety, they were told.

"It didn't take them long to find us," Cefe remembered. "We heard voices and footsteps coming quickly toward us. They opened the door, dragged us out, and beat us the whole way down the gangplank."

They should have given up. But that was when they decided to try the one thing they hadn't wanted to consider until then: going it alone. They would do it by blending in with the stevedores. They observed the men's work in detail, the shifts, how they chose who would help load which ship. For some time, the three friends worked the job straight, to win the trust of the foremen and the port workers, but also to learn the layout of the ships' holds and get a sense of where it would be best to hide. Ceferino remembered it as the hardest work he'd ever done— harder than working sheet metal in Barcelona or harvesting grapes in Bordeaux.

They handpicked the stevedores for every job. The call—that was the term they used at the docks—came three times a day: morning, afternoon, and night. A big group of hopefuls in berets would gather, milling around the foremen, who would stand at the feet of the ships and choose crews of fifteen men or fewer. And since loading or unloading a ship could take from eight to ten days, depending on the tonnage, Ceferino and his friends had time to study their options. The most delicate operation—transporting gold ingots by hand—required added security.

In principle, this was the worst time to hole up on board as a stowaway. Or maybe it wasn't . . .

"I didn't think twice. The very day when we had the most eyes on us was the one when I managed to get on this ship," he told the astonished sailor. "It was thanks to a robbery on the docks and the uproar that followed. I don't know if you heard the commotion. During the chaos, I took off running, and I could hear the bullets whiz past me. Then I saw the ramp leading up to the *Liberté*; it seemed to be telling me to try my luck. I crossed the deck without looking back, hid down in the hold, and you know the rest."

Ceferino knew nothing about the fate of his companions. He hoped they'd made it onto one of the other ships moored in the port. They'd agreed it was each man for himself, but the other two kept balking at it when the moment came. For him, at least, it had worked. Down in the hold of the *Liberté*, huddled among the cargo, he felt as if he were in the entrails of a giant whale: a whale that weighed fifty-one thousand tons, as Joe had told him, and was three hundred yards long and thirty-two yards wide.

He was no more than a drop of water in the middle of a storm.

But all through that storm, huddled in that claustrophobic make-shift cell, he could hear his father whispering in his ear, encouraging him: *Don't give up, son.* Thanks to those heartening words, and the memory of his father's stoicism during his own much more perilous time in captivity, Ceferino's lonely journey seemed milder, easier to bear.

And if he needed another nudge, all he had to do was reach a hand into his pocket and take his mother's photo from his wallet. His memory didn't have to drift too far back—and his situation, stuck there in transit, stirred up recollections like nothing else—for him to realize his time as a stowaway wasn't all that desperate. Yes, it felt like everything was moving too slowly, but he didn't lose hope, even when Joe confirmed that the captain had revised their schedule and the crossing would take longer than they'd expected. His only worry was that the kind sailor would get tired of helping him. Then he would be truly alone.

"You don't need to worry about that," Joe reassured him. "I'll take care of you till we get there."

Ceferino had lived his entire life thinking nothing was permanent, and he'd gotten used to not letting people or hard times disappoint him. He had an extraordinary resilience and a capacity to emerge from difficulties stronger than he'd been before, and since the sailor had exceeded all his expectations, he decided to trust the man, to trust that the winds would take him where he was meant to be. Slowly, slowly, he began to adapt to the rhythm of the voyage.

The boy thought calmly, slept calmly, and even ate calmly. As if he were savoring that varied repertory of foods the sailor snuck him. Apparently, he had a friend on the kitchen crew who pretended to look away while he gathered up the leftovers. The longer Cefe took to eat, the more time he spent with Joe, who was his only human contact.

"This ship won the Blue Riband in 1930. It was called *Europa* then and belonged to the German merchant marine."

"What's the Blue Riband?"

"The prize given to the ship that made the best time between Hamburg and New York. But the war ruined everything."

"What happened?"

"France got the ship as part of the war booty. They gutted it in the port and turned it into what it is now: something halfway between a cruise ship and a merchant ship. Practical but elegant at the same time, see. The *Liberté* is just another child of the war," Joe said, winking at him affectionately.

The sailor could see he was anxious.

"Don't sweat what you can't fix. Think of all the great things that are waiting for you. Remember?" Joe rolled up his sleeve and pointed at his tattoo. "You still don't know what this means?"

Ceferino shook his head.

"It's about freedom, kid. You can kick and scream all you want, but sooner or later, you've got to go out and get things done on your own. So chin up. You're about to see an entirely new world."

The days passed with stultifying slowness. But Ceferino was optimistic by nature and didn't let the weight of the past or his loneliness get him down. He had the chance to put his life in order, to learn he who was, and to figure out who he wanted to be.

Sometimes he heard the muffled voices of passengers. He amused himself by reconstructing their conversations, the relationships between the speakers, the excitement of their lives. He didn't imagine himself involved in the situation; instead, it was as if he were watching a film from the front row, chewing a chocolate bar like the one he'd devoured at the beginning of the trip. His love for film was his deepest secret. Ceferino was crazy about everything to do with the movies, and when he was younger, he had dreamed of becoming an actor. But that desire didn't last long; it had dwindled and then vanished when the realities of life brought him back down to earth. All his options passed through a single arrival point that he kept in his wallet, next to that photograph of his mother and his Spanish ID card: a wrinkled scrap of paper with an address dashed off hastily by hand, the home of the only family member he had in America, his uncle Ramón. He had copied it down himself from a letter his mother kept in an armoire in the dining room. Finding it was the last push he needed to run away.

One day, the voices outside the ship's hold were a little too clearly audible, distinct from those of the crew members who occasionally came down to where the goods were kept and made Ceferino realize he'd been right to hide. These voices came to him with a frightening clarity.

"Hear that?" The sailor didn't take long to come over and tell him to prick up his ears.

"It's . . . people talking?" he said, surprised.

Joe nodded with closed eyes.

"We should take our chances before the sun comes up, while it's still foggy and a lot of the passengers have gone up on deck."

"Take our chances doing what?"

"We're about to reach the port. New York. You made it."

He was a man of few words—though Ceferino's flimsy English couldn't handle many, anyway. He didn't know what to say, let alone what to do. But the sailor understood. He put a hand on the boy's shoulder to steady him. Partly because the waves were choppy on that stretch, but mainly because he needed Ceferino to pay attention to him one last time.

One last time before the ship's siren announced their entry into New York Bay, before the engines stopped, before the tugboats started pulling them toward land. Before Joe gave him a suitcase left behind by some passenger, along with a five-dollar bill—"A passenger without a suitcase looks suspicious, and the money will be enough for you to make it to your uncle's."

Before Ceferino emerged from his hideout to witness the broad morning sky, feeling the wind riffling through his hair and stroking his face, inviting him to mingle with the other travelers. Before he tried to answer the questions from the customs officials and the health inspectors who stood between him and the Promised Land. Before all this, Ceferino looked again at the man's tattoo, which now seemed to be speaking directly to him: *Growl you may, but go you must!*

"Now's when we go our own ways," the sailor said to him. "You know what you've got to do."

CHAPTER 2

That July morning in 1949, Ceferino Carrión was moved almost to tears by the sight of the big city rising up over the water. There was something both hypnotic and savage in that crescendoing image that seemed like a set from a movie. It wasn't the ship that was approaching New York, but the city that was swallowing the ship.

Dawn still hadn't broken, and the boy floated toward the heart of New York, eyes wide, overwhelmed by its dimensions. Not to mention the sea of cars and people coursing back and forth along Eighth Avenue, the name of which was the only thing he remembered from the directions Joe had given him to keep him from getting lost. He was shivering from head to toe and bathed in cold sweat. The transition from the cramped hideaway in the hold of the *Liberté* to his welcome before—or rather, behind—the Statue of Liberty filled him with a kind of vulnerable chill that wouldn't seem to fade—and yet he was convinced good fortune would smile upon him as soon as he figured out how to make it to the Bronx.

Clutching the little suitcase like a talisman, he gawked at the glimmering skyscrapers with their facades stretching infinitely upward, dotted with thousands of closed windows. No matter how far he looked, he couldn't see the ends of them, and they gave him vertigo. They were all sharp angles and immense dimensions, as if the city were a gawky adolescent still waiting to finish its growth spurt. Not daring to breathe too deeply, he held on to the one thing that was his and his alone—the suitcase—and kept his eyes on the scrap of paper with the address of his father's brother, Uncle Ramón, even though he knew it by heart.

2309 Arthur Avenue.

He looked at a crossing guard trying to establish some kind of order amid the endless vehicle and foot traffic: delivery vans, taxis that might screech to a halt at any moment, cars in bright colors and the occasional motorcycle jockeying for lanes, and very elegant men and women, taking cover from the summer sun with broad-brimmed hats or caps, waiting their turn to cross the wide street. There, in the middle of that multitude milling on the crosswalks and intersections, he felt alive. Pushed and shoved, but alive.

Ceferino waited for the absolute worst moment to approach the orchestra director in the blue uniform conducting that urban symphony.

"Bronx? Bus?" he asked with an unsure voice, showing the man the paper with the address.

The crossing guard read it and jerked his head a few times to one side. He was used to giving directions to people fresh off the boat with little knack for the language. He stressed his directions with very precise gestures and wrote the letter *D* on Ceferino's paper.

"D. Go down in the subway. The train for the Bronx is the D."

"D," Ceferino repeated slowly.

The cop nodded and motioned for him to keep going up the avenue, then gave him a sort of martial salute, touching his temple with the tips of his fingers.

To minimize the risk of getting lost along the way, Ceferino concentrated on finding the subway entrance, and only once he was downstairs did he let himself get distracted by the sights—in this case, another person waiting on the platform. A young black girl sitting on a bench, who didn't look lost the way he did. She was the first person he'd had time to observe at ease since arriving in the United States. He looked at her hair, pulled back in a bun, the same way his sister Angelines wore hers. He liked her bright face and her big, dark eyes, and her red lips seemed eminently kissable. Cefe was dying to say something to her, in spite of his limited English and his generally deplorable appearance. He smiled at her, as he did with every pretty girl he came across. He couldn't help it. Then he looked up and down the tracks, wondering which way the train would come from. When it appeared, the girl stood up—she'd been waiting for the same one. A gray-green beast with a red floor and red seats, the words "Sixth Avenue" in a black-and-white sign on its flank, it screeched metallically to a stop. Ceferino stepped back to let the girl enter first. He didn't understand the scathing glances of the passengers until he saw her sit down. Immediately, the whites around her got up and changed places.

He stepped on and showed the paper with the address to one of the passengers.

"Fordham Road," the man said, and then, louder, "FORDHAM ROAD." When Cefe tried to ask how long it would take to get there, the man told him to leave him be, in Spanish, with a strong American accent.

No matter. He was on the train, and he would get there eventually. Cefe sat next to the black girl and weathered the surly stares from his fellow riders. When she wouldn't meet his eyes, he looked out the windows, watching the passing of the stations with their colored tiles and the dark interior of the tunnel.

The train wound through the bowels of Manhattan and eventually came to his stop in the Bronx. Gone was the sea of skyscrapers, replaced by rows upon rows of no-longer-gargantuan buildings with zigzagging stairways on their facades. American flags flapped on most of the housefronts, and the bus stops and billboards seemed designed to clear up the boy's worries. An ad for Pepsi took him aback: it glowed on the roof of a building, a giant bottle cap flanked by two mammoth bottles. Everything in America looked big, deluxe, endless.

Everything but the narrow alleys and the occasional closed mind, apparently. What he'd seen on the train had upset him, but he didn't want to let any nastiness spoil this milestone, having his feet on the ground in this new land of opportunity that he was ready to take by storm. Little by little, his nervous sweat drained away, dried by the balmy air of summer.

Ceferino Carrión and his accidental suitcase were finally in the Bronx, in search of 2309 Arthur Avenue, apartment 4-2, the home of his uncle Ramón, which Cefe hoped to call home for a while, too. But first he ran into the building's superintendent, who was on her way out to run errands and seemed shocked when she saw the boy. She did a double take and squinted as if she couldn't believe her eyes.

"Justo Ramón?"

Cefe was confused. Who was Justo Ramón? He shook his head. "My name is Ceferino Carrión, and I'm looking for my uncle Ramón Carrión. Do you know if he lives here?"

"My baby!" María Buenavida exclaimed; she seemed to be holding back a maternal urge to hug him.

The one who didn't hold back, and who nearly crushed him to death, was his uncle Ramón, who jumped out, squeezed his hand, then pulled him into a bear hug, following it with a few thundering claps on the back.

"You're the spitting image of your father!" Ramón told him, smiling widely.

Ramón Carrión had more Cantabria than North America in him. He was a slender man with a slight hump at the top of his back; a narrow face, sunken and furrowed like a raisin; bushy eyebrows that barely revealed his eyes; and a gaze that strongly recalled Ceferino's father. He was a Carrión through and through. A widower with one son, Julio, the same age as Ceferino, Ramón had made a place for himself in that community as the owner of a small restaurant and bar, a simple establishment on the edge of the Quarry Ballfields frequented by working-class locals. At that hour, he had just returned from buying fruits and vegetables from Mr. Provenzano's store.

"I just got into the city. I brought your address with me all the way from Spain."

He showed him the wrinkled scrap of paper.

"Welcome home!"

And the two men hugged while beside them, María Buenavida murmured over the resemblance again: "Justo Ramón."

The bustling life of the Bronx suited Cefe. At times, that working-class city within a city reminded Ceferino of his neighborhood in Barcelona. Maybe it was the boisterous streets packed with bakeries, butchers' shops, hardware stores, seamstresses, and fruit stalls pouring out onto the sidewalk, offering their goods in crates piled up before the customers' eyes. Or maybe it was the abundance of bars and taverns where the neighbors gabbed over their beers—when they weren't having bull sessions and telling stories in the doorways.

"The Bronx has become home for the children of the Irish, Italians, Greeks, Poles, Germans, and Spanish people like us. We've been here twenty years now," Ramón explained to him. The borough had also gained a reputation as the part of New York with the most boxers, roughnecks, and gangsters per square foot. "But most of us are humble working people, with a strong feeling of community. We help each other out because we're one big family," he said.

Arthur Avenue was the main thoroughfare crossing through the Italian neighborhood. It was a broad street, full of life, fragrant with washing soap from the clothing hung on balcony clotheslines, dots of color against the gray buildings, and with the variety of spices whose scents wafted out of kitchen windows across the neighborhood.

Within days of arriving, Ceferino had his first shift in his uncle's restaurant. There was always something to do there, and the boy worked like crazy. There was barely a second's rest; days turned into weeks, weeks turned into months, and it wasn't long before he felt at home.

One night he fell asleep in the park while waiting for his cousin to accompany him home, and someone stole the few possessions he had on him, including his ID card. The next day, while Ceferino, Uncle Ramón, and Julio were trying to figure out what to do, María Buenavida came to them with a plan.

"Good morning," she said. "Sorry for barging in at this hour."

"No problem, María! You're always welcome in our house." Uncle Ramón offered her a chair and a place at the table with them. "Something going on? You feel like a coffee?"

"No, no, thanks." She sighed long and deep. "I'm here to make you a proposition."

"Do tell."

"Last night, Cefe told me how they stole his wallet."

"That's just what we were talking about," Ramón said.

"So I've been turning it over . . . and . . . it may sound crazy, and I know I shouldn't stick my nose into other people's business, the way my daughter always says. But I was thinking Cefe could use my son Justo's papers. Justo Ramón León. They're nearly identical. That could help him straighten things out."

The Jones-Shafroth Act, signed by President Woodrow Wilson in March 1917, granted full American citizenship to Puerto Ricans like María and her boy. But Justo Ramón León suffered from a debilitating illness that kept him confined to his grandmother's home in Old San Juan in Puerto Rico, and his mother had resigned herself to living without him.

"He'll never come to New York. Not to the Bronx, not to Arthur Avenue. If I do this for you, Cefe, in a way it's like I'm doing it for my boy."

"Mrs. Buenavida, I don't know what to say. Thank you. I owe you and your son."

"No, Cefe. You don't owe me anything. To me, you're another member of the family." She winked. "All I ask is that you live the life you want to live, because you're healthy and you can do so."

A few days later, Ceferino accompanied his uncle to report the theft of his papers and adopt a new identity with the authorities.

"What's your name, kid?" the officer asked.

"Justo Ramón León Buenavida," Ceferino responded without hesitation. The officer filled out the police report and took down a statement from Ramón Carrión, who acted as a witness to corroborate what had happened and verify that this young man without papers was who he said he was.

A temporary identification card recognized him for the first time as a citizen of the United States. And it was done. Cefe was Justo now, and he was safe.

A new name wasn't the only joy María Buenavida brought into Cefe's life. The same day Ceferino reported his theft at the police station, María's beautiful daughter, Eva María, was celebrating her twentieth birthday, and the Carrión family was invited to the feast, with all its sounds and aromas.

For weeks now, Ceferino and Eva María hadn't bothered to hide their feelings for one another, though they hadn't gone any further than ardent stares, pretty words, the occasional compliment. The boy had even mentioned her to his mother in one of the letters he tried to write her every week, in which he reported all the good things that were happening to him. Eva María was one of them. He couldn't wait to show her his new papers.

Cefe didn't think he would mention his change of identity to his mother. He felt he was betraying his father's memory by giving up his last name, but he was also aware of the many difficulties he'd spare himself by trading Carrión for León. In addition to his being in the United States illegally, there was also the inescapable fact that he remained on the run after dodging his call-up for military service in his home country. He needed to be practical, and if he had to take a new name, León at least was one that inspired confidence, reminding him of lions and their abundant courage. His first name was a different story—it just didn't feel like him. Ceferino was the only name he responded to.

The scent of garlic, pepper, and oregano coming up from the ground floor filled the stairwell to the top of the building. Mrs. Buenavida had made the *sofrito* for a rice dish she was baking in the oven along with ham garnished with bay leaf and olives. Also rising up from the ground floor were the sounds of music from the Mediterranean.

"It smells so good you can taste it," Uncle Ramón said to Mrs. Buenavida by way of greeting.

"It's *arroz con gandules*," the superintendent exclaimed proudly, all dolled up for the occasion.

An amused, quizzical look appeared on the man's face.

"*Gandules* are green tropical peas. It's a very old Boricua recipe."

"I thought you were from Puerto Rico."

"I am! My mother's a descendant of the first inhabitants of the island. And they were known as Boricuas, which means 'the people who eat crabs' in Taino."

"The things you learn!" Uncle Ramón smiled.

"That rice will make you want to lick your plate clean!" the superintendent said.

They greeted the birthday girl in the living room. As she did her rounds, she leaned over slightly to receive a kiss on the cheek from all those who had just arrived. She left Ceferino for last.

"Thanks for coming, Justo Ramón."

The boy hadn't expected her to call him by her brother's name, even though it was his name now.

"I wish you many more," he dared to say.

"Now that we're family . . . ," Eva said in a flippant tone.

"Don't joke about that. If I ever get the chance to go to Puerto Rico, I'll try and meet your brother. I'm very thankful to him."

Before he could add another word, the girl was off to talk with the rest of the attendees. It was her day, and more guests were coming in. Family, friends, other Puerto Ricans from the neighborhood, turning the ground-floor apartment into a small San Juan.

Suddenly the girl let out a scream, and Cefe whipped his head around. He turned just in time to see her leap into the arms of a tubby man standing in the doorway. He had a part in his hair, a mustache, and a smile on his face, arms loaded down with musical instruments.

"Baby!" The man put down his load to embrace her.

"Who's that?" Cefe asked.

"Miguelito Tito Arvelo," Julio replied. "He's a cousin of María's, and he plays with the Pérez Prado Orchestra and the Victoria Quartet."

Arvelo was accompanied by a guitarist and a maraca player, and soon they'd begun to liven up the party with Caribbean rhythms: congas, mambos, merengues. Between the music, the food, and the alcohol, everyone was having a great time. Ceferino, amused, watched from a corner, waiting for some attention from Eva María, who was also dancing and smiling profusely. She was happy, it was easy to see, attentive to everyone and captivating as always.

Eva María was neither tall nor petite, and although slender, she filled out the right parts of her sleeveless dress with its flower print. She wore her wavy hair cropped short; it was dark brown, like her big, round eyes. Ceferino couldn't look away from her small pink lips, which were grinning with contagious innocence. *It wouldn't take anything for me to fall in love with that girl,* he'd thought the first time he greeted her in the building's stairwell.

But then, he fell in love easily, no way around it. Chiqui, his youngest sister, constantly threw it in his face. Ceferino, who knew his limits, had learned to compensate for his small stature and modest physical attractions with other charms. It had thus far worked out well for him: he had an eternal infectious smile and a sincere and welcoming expression in his eyes, which were always pinned on whoever he spoke with. Cefe knew how to play on his good-boy image and his innate capacity to listen with unfeigned interest, both of which the girls always loved.

Eva María came over to him and smiled. "You want to dance?"

"Dance?" he responded uneasily.

"Now that you're Puerto Rican, you should let the music grab hold of you. Trust me," she whispered in his ear. "And look me in the eyes."

Ceferino grabbed her around the waist, and, as he would every time he had the chance to hold her tight, he wished he could keep her body close to him forever.

"You like living here?" the girl asked as they danced around the room.

"Absolutely! With Uncle Ramón and my cousin, it's like being back with my father and my older brother."

"You don't miss your family back in Spain?"

"I miss them all the time. I think about my sisters and my mother. I try to write home whenever I can so they won't worry about me."

It touched Eva María's heart to know the boy kept in touch with those he'd left behind. A few days later, she agreed to go to the movies with him and his cousin Julio, who also brought a date—Lara, a waitress from the restaurant who had been after him for some time. The four of them chose a film everyone had been talking about.

"It's a musical with Gene Kelly and Frank Sinatra. They told me it's amazing!" Julio said, trying to convince his cousin.

"What's it about?"

"Three sailors who get off in New York and have one day to see the city."

"Is it the movie or the company you're so excited about?"

His cousin didn't bother answering. It was obvious.

The night was splendid, though very cold. Lara and Julio couldn't help but belt out that famous melody that was constantly blaring from all the radio stations. Arm in arm, they emptied their lungs, singing "New York, New York."

Cefe and Eva María lingered behind the other two. Cefe took a chance and kissed her for the first time, just one of many kisses to come. A kiss with a hint of mustard from their movie-theater hot dogs. After they pulled apart, Eva María froze.

It's one of two things, Cefe thought. *Either she didn't like it, or she didn't see it coming.*

"A brother and sister shouldn't be kissing, it's against the laws of nature." Eva María smiled at him, eyes sparkling.

"You're not my sister, and I'm not your brother," he responded, relieved, and smiled back at her. "I just have his name. I'm Cefe, and don't forget it. For you, I'm Cefe." He winked at her.

When they caught up with their friends, Ceferino wore a conspicuous grin. He couldn't believe he had just laid a kiss on Eva María. He felt like the luckiest guy in New York.

"Was the ship you came to America on like the one in the movie?" Eva María asked him.

"Pretty much!" Ceferino said. "But the sailors didn't sing or dance." He laughed.

It had been a while since he'd thought about the trip. Or about Joe. Or about the dreams he'd had every day he was cooped up in the stinking, dark hold of the ship. *How fragile memory can be,* the boy thought.

"It's funny. In one day, these guys from the film manage to see all the sights of the city. Me, I've been living in New York for five months, and I've still never been to the Empire State Building, the Brooklyn Bridge, or Central Park . . . And I've only seen the Statue of Liberty from behind!"

"Well, there's one place you can check off your list," Julio said, turning toward him. "My father got tickets for the three of us to Madison Square Garden. We're going to go see the fights!"

The whole city was already talking about the upcoming match. Rocky Marciano, the Rock, fighting for the heavyweight title, was coming in at 17–0 against Carmine Vingo, the great hope from the Bronx. Both fighters were Italian Americans and shared a similar constitution, but Vingo was far taller and more muscular than Marciano.

Ceferino hadn't yet decided who was his favorite in the coming fight. He felt drawn to both boxers. He admired the discipline and bravery demanded by that sport, one that so many poor kids turned to as a way out of a life of crime. He had met a few boxers in the neighborhood, guys who found time to train despite their jobs, which were demanding enough. The little that Cefe knew about Marciano fascinated him, though he wasn't a true fan. Vingo's story was compelling, too, but it was one he was too well acquainted with, one that hit too close to home.

"Remember Renata? The cook at the restaurant?" Julio asked.

Ceferino nodded.

"Marciano's opponent is her kid. Carmine Vingo. We all call him Bingo Vingo. He just turned twenty. He's tall and strong, and he can box."

In the days before the event, Ceferino had been convinced that Bingo's courage and daring would be enough to topple Marciano. Inspired by the idea of overcoming the odds, which they felt was their own story as well, the boys left home headed for Madison Square Garden, ignoring the glacial cold on that December night, which vanished once they got inside beneath the spotlights, wedged in among the fans. More than nine thousand people had packed the stands in what had become boxing's cathedral to watch what everyone predicted would be an unforgettable bout.

Ceferino hadn't seen so many people in one place since he'd left the port and jumped into life in the city. His uncle Ramón watched him, amused. The older man remembered how he'd felt the first time he'd seen crowds like that. The Garden that night was deafening, filled with music and jubilation. Apart from Ceferino, there was hardly a person in the audience who wasn't shouting for one of the two boxers.

The boxers walked into the arena. Ceferino craned his neck to get a look. Julio was ecstatic, punching the air as if fighting some invisible adversary. The public shouted and whistled. Around the ring, the judges, the ring girls, and the doctors were making their final preparations. The audience roared when they announced Carmine's name. As the upstart, the one trying to beat the superstar, he walked out to the center and greeted the audience. He received a warm and uproarious reception in return: he was on his home turf. Everyone was also excited to see Rocky Marciano, who wore a black robe with his name embroidered in gold. He lowered his head to pass under the ropes and raised his arms to greet the masses.

"Rocky! Rocky! Rocky!"

Ceferino, squeezed in between his uncle and cousin, jumped out of his seat. He watched the bout with his heart pulled in both directions. Right away, Marciano took the initiative, and all Vingo could feel was the force of his rival's strikes. Ceferino was amazed at Bingo's capacity for recovery: he took every one of the Rock's punches without flinching. Marciano was putting on an astonishing display of strength and superiority, but Vingo still tried to give back as much as he got. The Rock was coming hard and fast. Vingo got hit, then tried to hit back. Both boxers were bleeding, with all sorts of cuts and bruises, but Vingo was by far the worse for wear, and no one understood how, tired as he was, he had held up through those first five rounds. He just wouldn't quit. Over and over, he fell to the canvas, but he kept getting back up.

At the opening of the sixth, Marciano hit him square in the jaw, making his head wrench around violently. A long *Oooh!* rang out, and then the crowd went silent as Carmine Vingo hit the floor. Neither the ref nor his cornermen could do anything to revive him. He didn't move, and the public watched in silence. A tragedy seemed imminent.

Vincent Nardiello, the Garden's doctor, jumped into the ring. He gave Vingo a shot of adrenaline to the heart, and that made him react. He stood up partway, stumbled for a few steps like a baby just learning to walk, and then collapsed. Was he dead, or just knocked out? Marciano didn't budge from his corner. The medic shouted for a stretcher to get the boxer to the hospital. The bout was over. The public filed out quietly, leaving Madison Square Garden with heavy hearts.

Neither Ceferino, Uncle Ramón, nor Julio dared utter a word. They couldn't erase the image of Renata's son lying on the floor. They went to St. Clare's Hospital, where Vingo had been taken, to give support to the family. At reception, they were greeted by a nun in a black habit and veil, with a white coif framing her face.

When they reached the landing of the second floor, a large crowd had already gathered around room 234. They were family members and neighbors, all of them with the same idea. Cefe hadn't guessed there would be so many people. He could count at least a dozen. Two Franciscan sisters made sure the people gathered next to the room didn't make too much noise and disturb the other patients. Cefe and his uncle pushed through the middle of the group and made their way inside.

Cefe's heart broke when he saw Renata, disconsolate in one corner of that filthy hospital room. She was crying like a baby, repeating as she looked at the bed where her son lay, "Ay, my Carmine! My poor son! All he wanted was to make a little money to marry Kitty! He was so excited to face his idol in Madison Square Garden. Damn you, Marciano!"

But Marciano would leave his mark one more time that night. Although everyone thought he had gone off to the dressing rooms, bruised but victorious, in fact he was shaken and saddened after seeing his hardy young adversary lying there unconscious. Instead of leaving the Garden and hiding out, he did something that honored his opponent. Marciano showed up at the hospital to pay his respects to Vingo's family.

When he arrived, accompanied by his manager, all murmuring and whispers ceased and a majestic silence fell over the crowd. They opened a path for the boxer to pass through. No one uttered a word. Cefe got goose bumps and could feel a knot in his stomach. Everyone was awed at the champ's gesture. Marciano was used to a crowd's eyes being pinned to his broad back; it was nothing new for him. Without saying anything, he went in and knelt by Renata, who was praying for Carmine's life while she waited for news from Dr. Nardiello, who had taken care of him from the moment he'd been knocked unconscious. She prayed he would reassure her. Lying there in that bed, Vingo was in the toughest and most decisive fight of his short career.

When Marciano knelt down next to the weeping mother, the wrath vanished from the woman's face. She embraced the boxer but didn't even try to suppress her grief. The champion stroked her hair and whispered a few words in her ear that only she could hear.

Uncle Ramón looked at his son and at Cefe. They agreed in silence to leave the hospital. Crestfallen, they crossed Hell's Kitchen and traveled back up to the Bronx without a word. Cefe couldn't shake his bewilderment. The lesson from what he'd seen in the Garden might have been that you couldn't stand up to an established power, that the simple people who dream of one day making it into the pantheon, of becoming stars, could never do so. But no. He refused to believe that. He was like Vingo: nothing would stop him, nothing would make him flinch. But like Vingo, he would have to fight—that much was clear. He would have to work hard and never let down his guard.

By the time they made it back home, it was late, but María Buenavida knocked on their door, frantic.

"Cefe! This afternoon a letter came for you."

"From my mother? From Barcelona?"

Ceferino was shocked to see the seal of the Spanish Ministry of Defense. He had to read the letter three times before he could utter the news aloud.

"What does it say?" Julio asked impatiently.

"Someone told Franco's authorities I'm a deserter," he whispered.

"Bastards!" his uncle said.

"I ran away to stay out of the army, and now they're telling me I have to go back." He paused. "What I don't get, what I can't figure out, is how they found me. I hope no one in my family's in trouble."

Ceferino's blood froze when he remembered his father's time in prison.

"I can't stay here. They could come for me anytime and make me go back to Spain."

He didn't know what to do. He felt lost. Or worse, defeated, a sensation he thought he'd left behind long ago.

The idea of being repatriated, of going back, of defeat, accompanied him night and day, but he also knew he couldn't give up now. He'd done the hardest part: he had made it here, a stowaway, all the way into the United States, changing his identity. He had to keep pushing ahead!

He remembered the day he had seen New York from the deck of the ship, as imposing and powerful as the dreams of the recent arrivals, which no obstacle could defeat. America meant the chance at another life, at being reborn. It was true that after five months, he didn't have much to show for his time here—not yet, anyway—and he sometimes felt he was stagnating, spinning his wheels. But now, with his new identity, a whole range of possibilities had opened up to him.

Ceferino said nothing. His uncle Ramón stayed silent as well.

It seemed his time there was at an end, but he knew his adventure in America wasn't over.

Growl you may, but go you must!

The message of that sailor's tattoo resounded in his head. He thought it over, along with the words of his father's he remembered so well: *You make your choices. You and you alone.* He knew the path he would have to take even if he wasn't sure yet where it led. New York was just a stage in a journey that was far from over.

That night, Eva María showed up in the darkness of their secret meeting place behind their apartment building. The wrought-iron frame of the staircase protected them from prying eyes.

"Eva María." Ceferino's voice was more subdued than usual.

"My mother told me about your letter from Spain."

They hugged.

"I have to go."

"But where will you go?"

When they'd had quiet moments, the young lovers had made lists of the projects they wanted to share. Eva María's dream was to become a teacher; she studied at night, determined to make it. Ceferino's was to climb the ladder from helping out in his uncle's restaurant to driving a taxi, and finally to running his own business. But for some time now, the girl had also noticed how excited her boyfriend got about Hollywood. When they went to the movies, she would talk about the characters and their stories, while Ceferino would carry on about what the lives of the *actors* must be like—he wanted to be loved and admired like them. And after the night of that fight at the Garden, Cefe had to admit that he longed for the kind of prestige and dignity Rocky Marciano enjoyed.

"Will you go to California?" she asked.

Cefe nodded silently. It was the only place he wanted to be, other than right there, in the stairwell with her.

Eva María threw her arms around his neck and hugged him tight. She didn't want to stand in his way. She knew, even if he hadn't said so, that in his heart he was already gone. Without her. They held back their tears, like promises that couldn't be kept, as their warm bodies embraced in the night . . . Suddenly, Eva María pulled away from Ceferino, just far enough to be able to hand him something.

"I want you to take this." She showed him a triangular stone with human features that she wore around her neck. "It's a *cemí*. In Taino it means 'angel,'" she explained. "It was my grandmother's; her ancestors were Taino. She gave it to me to protect me on the sea voyage that took me here from our country. It will help you, too. I want you to have it." And she took it off to give it to him.

Her hands trembled. Ceferino accepted the gift, moved.

A shiver ran up his spine, because he knew there was no guarantee they'd see each other again. A jumble of feelings buffeted him inside.

That night in December 1949, Ceferino Carrión made a decision. Or, more accurately, a date with destiny.

He had come this far already, hadn't he? He was convinced he was made of the same stuff as Carmine Vingo, but also that he could be like Rocky Marciano. Nothing was going to hold him back, stop him, keep him from his goal. He would win by points and would get the knockout, too, even if it meant he had to stay alert and on his toes.

The next morning Cefe put his most prized possessions in his suitcase from the *Liberté*. He caressed the *cemí* he'd hung around his neck and said goodbye to his family, the Carrións, and to the Buenavidas. Then he went straight to the army enlistment office downtown, close to Wall Street, to fill out his selective-service papers.

At the Greyhound terminal behind Penn Station, he bought a bus ticket to Los Angeles. *One way.*

Before getting settled in his seat, he had time to see the front page of a newspaper, which showed a photo of Carmine Vingo with his thumb raised, surrounded by nurses at St. Clare's. *From KO to OK,* ran the headline. Carmine had come out of his coma, and though the aftereffects would keep him out of the ring forever, Renata's boy had pulled through.

Now it was Ceferino Carrión's turn to chase destiny.

CHAPTER 3

On the West Coast, in the summer of 1950, it wasn't just the high temperatures eating away at Cefe's spirits. The added anxiety of the Korean War was terrifying the entire country, as the headlines reminded Ceferino every day, much to his consternation. The shadow of war had followed him ever since he had left Spain, and news of this kind affected him deeply. Then, a few days ago, he'd received his enlistment papers.

Ceferino was working the bar at Maxwell Coffee House, a café on Hollywood Boulevard, fretting about that faraway conflict that he, as a Spanish immigrant without any military calling whatsoever, neither understood nor felt a part of. He asked himself impatiently if America really needed more heroes in a far-off corner of Asia.

Heroes like him—not even an American. Or was he? He had his doubts. Who was he really? The citizenship he had so yearned for no longer gave him a refuge if it meant he had to fight in a war, this time for a country that wasn't even his own. He had suffered the aftermath of armed conflict in the flesh, had seen how it had made his family suffer. Now that he'd made it this far, now that he was comfortable with all the opportunities California offered at his feet, he didn't want to run away again. Let alone go back home.

Maybe, he repeated to himself over and over, trying to make himself believe it, *maybe this is all just a mirage.* Perhaps California wasn't the paradise he'd described to his uncle Ramón, who would send word on to his mother by letter, the only safe way to communicate with his family since the Spanish authorities could be intercepting Ceferino's mail. Once a month he talked to Ramón on the phone; he told his uncle all the humdrum details of his day-to-day life, and his uncle wrote it all down and passed it on to Cefe's mother. Those melancholic conversations left Ceferino glum for the rest of the day. He was no longer so sure what he was doing there or where he was headed. He didn't understand how his life had grown so complicated, when all he wanted was to be *someone*. To triumph.

Soon it would be six months since he'd arrived in Hollywood, which he quickly realized wasn't like the Hollywood he'd seen in magazines. He met wannabes just like him, men and women who had come from all over and would take any job—jobs like his, boring, dead-end jobs you could find in any corner of the world—so long as the schedule let them show up at the studios for auditions, be reachable by phone, and have enough free time for singing and acting classes . . . or anything else that might catch the attention of a talent scout.

Now that the army was on his tail, he felt all his aspirations and dreams for the big screen pulling away from him, before he'd even made any headway. In September, he would have to show up on the base in Sacramento. There wasn't much time to think, to decide, to find a workable solution. He didn't want to go on worrying. When the moment came, he would act.

"Hey, kid."

Ceferino was startled out of his spiral of dread. One of the café's usual customers, a guy who always sat at the corner table, was trying conspicuously to get his attention.

"Yeah, you!"

The man was beckoning him with an index finger, and Cefe hustled over to him. He was tubby and bald and had a shadow of a mustache under his nose. Ceferino hadn't seen him come in. As usual, the man was wearing a three-piece suit—this time a very white one—and a green shirt and a tie with yellow flowers that made the entire combination garish.

"Sit down a minute," he said.

"I'm sorry, sir, I'm working."

Ceferino preferred to remain standing, and not just for the sake of formality. There was something about this guy that he didn't trust.

"Of course," the man agreed, sarcastic, and leaned back in his seat. "I've had my eye on you for days. I like how you treat the customers."

"Thank you, sir."

"The other day I saw you waiting on Jorge Negrete himself, and doing a hell of a job, too. I reckon you two were talking in Spanish, right?"

Ceferino nodded.

"You don't hear that language too much around this part of the city . . ." The man suddenly seemed to notice Ceferino's discomfort. "May I introduce myself?"

With a cordial expression, he pulled a card from his coat pocket and handed it to Cefe. *José Durán, Artist Representation*. Ceferino's eyes showed interest for the first time.

"Now do you want to sit down?"

Naturally, he did. That day, which had begun with the dreadful shadow of war bearing down, now brightened up with the unexpected proposition the man was about to make him.

"Like I said, I've been watching you. You've got initiative, kid, you're sharp, people like you right off the bat, you've got that thing the French call . . . what's the word . . ."

"Du charme?" Ceferino offered.

"Exactly." He nodded, pleased. "Sharp as a tack. I'm convinced you and I could do interesting things together. I hope you don't feel too attached to your waiter job."

Ceferino shook his head.

"My agency represents artists internationally, and, as you must know, Hollywood is the center of the world when it comes to show business," he said, his voice getting louder as he pointed one finger toward the ceiling. "From your conversation with Negrete, I guess you know the Cansinos."

"Yes. I go to the Cansinos' flamenco school. It's close by, just around the corner," Ceferino told him.

"You must know that Eduardo Cansino is Rita Hayworth's father," Mr. Durán said.

Ceferino nodded enthusiastically. "Yes, she comes whenever she can."

"You like Rita?" Durán asked him mockingly.

"Eh . . . there's someone else I like better."

Ceferino shared a run-down bungalow with a guy and a girl, both from towns with unpronounceable names; they both went to Eduardo Cansino's dance school. Cefe dropped in now and then, and it was there that he had met the most captivating woman he'd ever seen in his life: Melita Cansino, Rita's cousin. She was a dancer in the studio, and he was head over heels for her. They had gone once or twice to a bar packed with people dreaming of being stars. And despite their differences, there were things about her—her face, her smile, especially the way she danced—that reminded him of Eva María. When Melita gathered her long black hair back into a ponytail, he felt a strong pull toward her, perhaps stronger than anything he had felt in the past. She was pure energy and passion. She would tug up the flounces on her skirt and dance. And dance and dance. When she did, Ceferino let himself be carried away by the spell for an eternity, bewitched by her sensual movements.

"If you know your way around that world, then you must have heard of Antonio and Rosario, too."

Mr. Durán spread a poster in front of him, unrolling it across the table. It showed a pair of dancers done up in flamenco dress.

"Yeah, I know them," Ceferino said, nodding.

"They're Andalusians and they're making a name for themselves all over the world. They've toured in South America. Mexico, Peru, Venezuela, Argentina . . . Not long ago, they had a billing at Carnegie Hall in New York. They've danced in the theater on the Champs-Élysées in Paris, at festivals in Scotland, Holland, and Italy, and in Spain, of course."

Ceferino's eyes were on fire.

"I've been following them for some time now," the agent continued, "so remember how not too long ago, the Americans were going crazy for the Dancing Cansinos—I mean Eduardo and his daughter Margarita, the one everyone calls Rita Hayworth, as you know . . ." The man swiped his hand through the air, as though chasing off a fly. "Well, I figure the moment's come for Antonio and Rosario to make their name in Hollywood."

Ceferino had held his breath throughout that perilous torrent of words: *Spain, triumph, Hollywood.* But before he could ask a question that would quell the fear welling up inside him, Durán laid out his plan:

"I want you to help me convince Antonio and Rosario to come here." Durán moved his head energetically as he spoke these words.

"Me?" Cefe's emotions, equal parts dread and joy, were so overwhelming, he didn't know what to say.

"I want them to come to Hollywood to make a film. I have contacts in the industry that I know would interest them. You could go to Spain using my name, offer them a contract, and . . ."

Durán smiled, revealing a row of very white teeth, save for one that stuck out conspicuously. Ceferino stared at that swatch of gold with its timid brilliance, like a spark. A very brief spark.

"So, what do you say? You can't reject an offer like this!"

It didn't matter that he had no experience in business, let alone the kind being proposed now, because one thing was true: Ceferino Carrión hadn't been put on this earth to turn down an opportunity.

Much less one as exciting as this one, traveling the world as a bona fide film professional, getting to see Spain again, and putting some distance, at least for now, between himself and the dangerous question of Korea. He told himself it was work, not fear, that was pushing him back to Spain—maybe he didn't have a job in Spain per se, but he was going there with a mission, a purpose, even if he had to do it undercover. And Justo León's papers would allow him to thwart—momentarily—Franco and his military justice.

When opportunity knocks, you've got to answer, Cefe thought. This was the first real door that had opened for him in Hollywood. But that door had been opened by a man who was more traveling salesman than showbiz magnate. Without nailing down any financial details, with nothing but the money for a round-trip ticket and a slim budget for expenses, the boy went down to the Los Angeles passport office the next day to apply for his visa. A week later, he was headed for Gibraltar on the *Saturnia*, a ship very similar to the *Liberté*, but on a journey as different as possible from that one a year earlier—even if the feeling of breaking the rules was the same. This time he wasn't a stowaway, but a deserter. Ceferino Carrión, traveling with his first US passport under the name Justo Ramón León, consoled himself with a thought as encouraging as it was dubious: *What if everything works out right?*

The journey was a smooth one—the furthest thing from his first horrifying crossing, huddled hidden down in the hold, scavenging for scraps. His persistent faith in his own good luck took him from Gibraltar to Málaga and on to Madrid, on the hunt for Antonio and Rosario, who were touring with a new show. The only thing he knew for sure was that they would make a stop in the capital at some point. It was his first time there, but he was nervous about sticking around. When he got out at Estación del Norte, he asked the way to the theater, and a passerby gave him directions to the Teatro Real, next to the Plaza de la Ópera.

To his surprise, he found a decrepit building, beautiful but boarded up. Someone told him it had been closed down since 1925—the work on Madrid's metro had damaged the foundations, and then it had suffered an explosion during the war. Further inquiries revealed that the dancers were in Barcelona, not Madrid. The place he'd been harboring in his mind and heart: Barcelona.

Barcelona! When he heard the name of his hometown, Ceferino felt a shiver. Immediately he felt the urge to call home to tell them he would be showing up the next day. He wasn't sure if he should, he didn't want to jinx himself. He didn't know if his voice would be steady enough to give them the good news.

"Hello?"

His suspicions had been right. His vertigo, his shakes, the relentless pounding of his heart left him speechless.

"Hello?!" the voice on the other end repeated impatiently. It was his sister Ana—Chiqui, as he called her, the little one, the youngest of nine (or really of eight, since his older brother José had died).

For several seconds, his welling emotions crowded out the words, and he struggled to unravel the knot in his throat.

"Chiqui!" Ceferino finally shouted.

And then there was a silence.

"Cebollita? Is it you, Cebollita?"

His nickname, Cebollita, little onion—they had always called him that, but not because he made people cry. No, it was the way he looked. Skinny and small-framed, like a scallion, pale and tender, with a round head.

"Yes, it's me!" Cefe crackled explosively, his nerves on edge. "Chiqui, I'm in Madrid, and I'll catch the train to Barcelona tomorrow. I'm coming to see you! I'm so excited . . ."

"Cefe, I can't believe it's you," Ana said in a strained tone, her euphoria seemingly cut short in a way that unsettled her brother.

After almost three years apart, exchanging information only sporadically, all Ana managed to tell him was "You can't come." There was no other sound but the usual static of a long-distance phone call.

"Why?" He didn't understand his sister's refusal.

"You won't be safe here. If they see you, they'll tell the authorities. It's not worth it, Cefe!" Chiqui insisted. "It's too risky."

"But I want to see you!" he protested.

"And we want to see you!" his sister assured him with a catch in her voice. "And if things were different, this would be the perfect time."

"Why?"

"Conchi's getting married this Saturday!" she told him, elated, despite her anguish, to share the news about their sister.

"What are you saying? How can I come to Barcelona and let a moment like that slip by me?" he insisted.

"You know what, Cefe? To hell with it! You come see us and we'll work out the rest."

Ceferino arrived at Barcelona's Estación de Francia at night, making it easier to get to his house without being seen. Being there stirred up those memories of the day his family moved to the Catalan capital after Santander, the city where he was born, had burned down. One of his oldest memories was also one of the most terrifying. Saturday, February 15, 1941. The night of the fire.

Ceferino was thirteen years old the night his parents woke the children to rush them out of bed. The historic center of Santander was burning, and they had to be ready for whatever might come. The Carrión family lived just a few yards from the Calle Cádiz, where everything had started. *Hell on earth*, the headlines called it in the following days, keeping a running tab of the destruction. The worst damage included the melting of the bells at the cathedral and the destruction of two rows of houses, not to mention the entire Hotel Victoria being reduced to ashes.

That whole day, a powerful wind had blown, making even walking difficult. Cefe's father hadn't gone to work; the fishing fleet had stayed moored in the port, dodging roof tiles, tree branches, electric cables, and lampposts that dropped down around them from the seaside promenade. They and their neighbors had long feared such a thing might happen: one spark from a stove shooting up a chimney and landing on one of the wood houses in that humble quarter was all it would take to reduce it to ashes. And that was exactly what happened, right there in the heart of the city.

The family shut themselves up at home, glued to the father's radio, listening to reports from a ship, the *Canarias*, that had anchored with supplies in the bay, responding to the news: *Santander is burning, Santander is burning,* repeated over and over. The family sat there in the dark paralyzed, hearts pounding, until their mother made the providential decision that they would flee the inferno. Ceferino remembered how they had to cover their faces because the fountain of flames was showering embers onto the wooden roofs of the Old Town. The narrow streets channeled the gusts of wind, intensifying them so the flames spread even faster.

They passed by the Café Boulevard, now a makeshift operations center where officials tried to control the flames. All the powers that be had gathered there. *One jet of fire could have burned them to a crisp and sent each and every one of them to hell,* Ceferino thought with rancor. Those assembled included the civil governor, the provincial party leader, the military governor, the infantry colonel, the president of the congress, the delegate for public order, and the mayor. They decreed a state of emergency, as if they were at war. In the morning, an enormous boom surprised Ceferino and his family—it sounded like an earthquake, so powerful it knocked them off balance. Later they learned the town had used dynamite to make a firebreak elsewhere in the city. Detachments of firemen came from all over Spain, and miraculously, only one person died in the tragedy: a man from their ranks, a firefighter from Madrid.

It wasn't until Monday morning that the wind died down and the fire could finally be put out. It left a scar that would mark the city, as well as the life of the Carrión family, forever.

That was when their father decided they would go to Barcelona. They could recover there, and he would be able to find work in the port. Unfortunately, soon after they moved, the war called him and José, Ceferino's older brother, up for service.

Now, exiting the Estación de Francia amid the shadows, Cefe couldn't help but retrace in his mind the path his family had taken after their arrival at the Catalan capital. He could taste the smoke in his throat, and fear pulsed through his body once again. It took more than a year for them to set down roots in their new city. And now Cefe felt like he was coming home, flooded with impressions, memories, long-dormant experiences brought back to startling life.

He took his usual route toward the district of Clot. As he got closer to the Carrión household, near the parish of Sant Martí, the urge to see his mother and siblings grew overwhelming. How frustrated he felt during that phone call when his sister told him it wasn't safe for him to come home! All he could do was stare at their building from the street. *The walls have eyes and ears,* his sister had told him.

Once he had settled in, he called her again and asked how they could meet. To his surprise, his family had taken care of everything.

"The priest, Father Ramon Torné, agreed to change the location of the wedding when Mama explained your situation to him," she had said. "It will be at the Church of Belén, on the Carrer del Carme, next to the Rambla. You can hide upstairs in the church, where the choir usually sits. There won't be anyone else there, just you."

"How do I get in?" Cefe asked.

"Take the street perpendicular to Carme, Carrer d'en Xuclá. Go to Granja Viader—remember it?" Cefe murmured an almost inaudible *yes.* "Ask for Mercè, the owner."

"The owner?" he asked, a bit unsettled.

"She's a friend, don't worry. She'll let you go through her courtyard, which leads to the Church of Belén. Once you're there, go to the sacristy and up to the choir loft before we arrive. Understood?"

"Of course. I'll be there!"

The night was hot, but Ceferino was still trembling from the sight of their building. He spent the night at a pension on Carrer dels Tallers. The next morning, he got up early and went out, looking for the finest clothes he could find to wear to his sister's wedding. *Manners are manners.* He didn't care that no one would see him. He ventured out and bought a navy-blue suit, a paisley tie, and a white kerchief that poked out of the pocket of his jacket and matched his shirt and the tips of his shoes.

He took Carrer de les Ramelleres toward Granja Viader. He strolled slowly, enjoying the feeling of being in his old city again. He walked into one of the florists' shops that had been the former homes of the *ramelleres*, the women who sold bouquets on the Rambla, and bought a bundle of roses for the bride. He put one bloom in the buttonhole of his jacket.

He had decided to have breakfast at Granja Viader, and he already knew what he would order: a cup of hot chocolate and some ladyfingers. When he stepped through the front door onto the cracked ceramic tiles, the intense scent of chocolate welcomed him. That sweet aroma called forth another memory, leading him back in time to an afternoon on Saint Joseph's Day when his parents had taken him and his brothers and sisters there for a snack. They were celebrating the name day of his older brother, grieving for him in his absence. Cefe loved the dessert that bore the boy's name—*crema catalana*, also known as *crema de San José*—and gulped it down while the other children slurped the melted chocolate in their cups.

Ceferino grazed the marble tabletops with his fingertips, and settled into one of the wooden chairs he'd found so uncomfortable as a boy. He glanced around, trying to call up more memories of that afternoon, the happy ones as well as the bitter, in a melancholy daydream that no amount of pastry, cream cheese with honey, *crema catalana*, or the countless shapes and flavors of the cakes and tarts behind the glass could sweeten. He missed his family—his mother, his siblings—and seated there, bouquet in hand, his longing grew even stronger. His eyes misted over, and little by little, so did the images of that long-ago afternoon.

Cefe didn't ask for the owner until he had finished his order and licked the sugar and chocolate from his fingertips and mustache. Señora Mercè came out from the back of the shop and greeted and chatted with a half dozen customers before stopping at Ceferino's table. Her face was stern until she saw the flowers on the table and the rose in his lapel, and then she broke into a generous smile.

"You're Cefe, Conchi's brother, right?" she asked in a soft, delicate voice that clashed with her staid appearance. "They tell me you've been overseas for a year, right?"

Cefe, trembling inside, nodded in response to the two questions. But the owner put him at ease, responding with her kindest smile.

"Follow me!" she said with a wink.

That roguish, knowing gesture made Ceferino's stiff nerves melt like the chocolate still smeared inside his cup.

They walked swiftly to the back of the shop, and Señora Mercè guided him outside, toward the courtyard of the church. They passed through the dairy where the employees made the whipped cream every day—wrapping it in cabbage leaves for customers to take it home—as well as butter, cottage cheese, flan, *crema catalana*, *arroz con leche*, and the star of the show, the chocolate.

"See that?" The owner of Granja Viader pointed out some stainless-steel tanks. "This is where all the chocolate for your sister's wedding will come from. I wanted to do something nice for your family, since I can't be at the ceremony."

The woman crossed the courtyard with him toward the church. She stopped in front of a metal gate with a rudimentary knocker and pointed at the run-down, decaying building—the sacristy of the Church of Belén. Now Señora Mercè took leave of a grateful Ceferino.

"I wish your sister all the happiness in the world. I'm glad I could do this for her."

Now he had to continue on his own. Cefe took a stone walkway to a nondescript door—two flaps of metal that gave no resistance when he opened them. He was surprised that entering the church was so easy.

Tenuous rays of light filtered in through the windows, and the scent of burnt wax drew him inside, where a warm silence reigned. Cefe crossed himself respectfully in front of a statue of the Virgin and left the bouquet of flowers at the foot of the altar where his sister would say yes to her future husband. He turned, looked up, and saw the benches in the choir loft. He walked up the nave toward it, passing the chapels of the Adoration, the Sacred Heart, the Virgin of Carmen, and the Virgin of the Abandoned and climbing the spiral staircase to his hideout. Once there, he waited patiently in the shadows for the entourage to arrive.

In that withdrawn, silent space, thoughts and memories of his father and his brother—who would, along with him, be the notable absences from the festivities—rose up inevitably before him. He took a deep breath, closed his eyes, and went back through the years, to just after the events that had turned their lives upside down.

A noise outside brought him back to reality. He heard the doors open and the murmur of guests entering and settling down on the benches. He crept over to the parapet and peeked down, trying to make out the members of his family. He didn't want to lose a single detail of the ceremony, the bride and groom, his family, the treading of the new shoes on the old, cracked floor creaking beneath their feet. So close, and at the same time so far away. He longed to go down and embrace them all, but he stayed put. His mother, his brother, his sisters, even the beautiful, beaming bride glanced furtively toward the shadows in the choir in turn, hoping to glimpse some slight movement that would reassure them Cefe was there.

"Finally. My prayers have been answered."

A familiar voice made him turn around, startled. It was Pedro, one of the friends he had fled to France with, sneaking into the choir stealthy as a fox sticking its muzzle into the henhouse.

"Pedro!" he whispered.

"Cefe! I knew it! What brings you here?"

"What do you think? I'm here for Conchi's wedding. You?"

"Fernando, the groom, invited me. He's my cousin, remember?" Pedro smiled, approaching him with a bizarre calm.

But Ceferino could sense the tension in his body and declined to embrace him.

"Look at you! Dressed to the nines," Pedro hissed sardonically. "Now I see why your mother and sisters were staring up here all nervous."

"I don't understand . . ."

"You won't get away this time. You'll pay for what you did to us."

"Me? What did I do?"

"You left us high and dry, Cefe!" Pedro reproached him. "Back there in Le Havre!"

"You listen to me, Pedro," he replied, irritated but not raising his voice. "We all decided to strike out on our own. Every man for himself. Then I hear you and Jaime teamed up again. That's got nothing to do with me. Remember? We agreed to meet in America, and then we bolted! Without looking back."

Pedro looked at him with fire in his eyes, but he didn't respond.

"You can blame fate for whatever happened to you," Cefe went on. "Is it my fault if you took the wrong boat and wound up in Guatemala instead of the USA?"

"You knew something, and you didn't tell us. Otherwise, how did you get to New York and we didn't?"

"Don't talk like an idiot! I got lucky, that's all."

"Look, Cefe, don't get smart with me. I've got you over a barrel," Pedro threatened him, raising a fist.

"What? You're gonna turn me in?"

Just as he uttered these words, Ceferino realized that was precisely what his old friend had already done. He could tell by the smug and hateful expression on Pedro's face. There was no doubt: he was the one who had ratted Cefe out to the Spanish authorities.

"Pedro . . . How could you do this?"

"Give me one reason why I shouldn't run and tell them where you are this very second. It would get me in good with the governor. I've got nothing, absolutely nothing to lose. The opposite, come to think of it."

"Now I see . . ." Cefe suddenly understood everything. "You never got over the fact that I made it to New York, right? That's what it is, no? Envy, it's eating you up inside, Pedro. And you can't even live with it, let alone be happy for me. You think making my life and my family's life impossible will make you feel better? You'll get what you want that way? What do you think will come of it? Ask yourself that."

Pedro flopped down on one of the benches, squeezed his temples in his hands, took a deep breath, and started crying. His tears were muffled by the cheering and shouts of "Long live the bride and groom!" that rose upward into the choir of the church.

Ceferino walked out of the shadows and over to the parapet to watch the entourage file out toward the Rambla. He suppressed the urge to shout in despair. When he looked at his miserable former friend, Cefe's heart filled with sorrow, rage, and disgust, and he left him there, taking the stairs and exiting through the main door. He mingled with the invitees and passersby, stopping to see the newlyweds. He wanted to join his family, if only to exchange a glance, but they were several yards away. All he could see were their outlines. They were a pleasing sight in their elegant clothes.

He didn't even get the chance to say goodbye.

He walked with his head down to the Teatro de la Comedia, on the corner of Gran Via and Passeig de Gràcia. The trip seemed to be nothing but a heap of shattered illusions. He tried to concentrate on how he might arrange a meeting with Antonio and Rosario, since they were the reason he had come to Spain. But his heart was heavy.

In Madrid, he'd learned that the dancers had gone to Barcelona as part of the repertory for Buero Vallejo's *Story of a Stairway*. That night's performance wouldn't start for several hours, so after arriving at the theater, he waited by the side door leading to the actors' dressing rooms. He hadn't prepared any remarks—he didn't think he needed to. The mere prospect of making a movie in Hollywood would be enough to entice anyone, he assumed.

Leaning against the wall, Ceferino lit a cigarette. He had just taken a drag when a taxi pulled up in front of him. Out stepped a man, very handsome and elegant in fine clothes, a beautiful silk tie knotted loosely around his neck. His skin was dark and luminous; his hair was black, meticulously combed back, and gleaming; his eyes were dark and seductive. It was Antonio. There was no doubt about it. Ceferino could confirm what he'd already heard: this fellow could win over men and women alike.

"Good afternoon!" Cefe stretched out his hand, putting on his best smile. "Antonio, the dancer?"

"That's right," the artist responded, his curiosity aroused.

Ceferino introduced himself as Justo León, a representative of the Durán Agency, which offered artist representation at the international level.

"I'm from Hollywood," he added, trying to entice the dancer. "Do you have time for a word with me?"

"Of course! But since you've come this far, you won't mind if we talk after the show, no? I'll wait for you in the dressing room, all right?" The man was pleasant but couldn't hide the vanity in his tone.

Cefe agreed and walked around to the box office to buy a ticket. He'd be able to make his arguments more persuasively if he knew the spectacle firsthand. It would look more professional.

But when the show started and Elena Salvador stepped onto the stage—playing Urbano's wife, Carmen, who is forced to meet in secret with her lover, Fernando—Ceferino lost his breath. His pupils dilated, his heart started pounding, and he could feel his body temperature rising. Every time she came onstage, Ceferino was mesmerized: by her voice, her eyes, her body. He didn't know if it was love at first sight, but he was struck.

Ceferino had heard it said that when you fall in love like that, it's because that person was your lover in another life. Maybe it was true, maybe not, but regardless, this woman aroused a nearly uncontrollable feeling in him, an intense emotional and sexual attraction, an impulse that drove him toward her. He had just enough time to rush back to the florist on Carrer de les Ramelleres and send flowers to her dressing room with a note that read, *I feel like Fernando. I just hope you don't have an Urbano in your life. Yours truly, Justo León.*

A few weeks later, there was a call at the Carrión household.

"Hello. Is this the residence of Ceferino Carrión?" a woman's soft voice asked.

"Yes, who's calling?" Chelo replied.

"I'm a friend of his. Who am I speaking with?"

"I'm his sister," Chelo said stiffly. "Who do I have the pleasure of—" Before she could finish the sentence, she had her answer.

Chelo was shocked when she heard the famous actress's name. What could that leading lady of the stage have to do with Cefe?

"I'm calling to tell you that your brother . . . Well, if you could come by to get the things Cefe left behind, he had to go back to the US. The army called him up for the war—the war in Korea."

The call didn't stretch on much longer, just enough for Elena to give an address where they could pick up the suitcases containing Cefe's knickknacks and clothing, a few keepsakes that his family would hold on to that were all they had left of him. Cefe, son and brother, after that unforgettable wedding day of September 2, 1950, disappeared from their lives again, this time forever and ever. Or so they thought.

On the deck of the ship, Ceferino felt nausea, but it wasn't from the rocking of the waves. The drops of salt water splashed his face and cooled his thoughts. The journey felt heavy with meaning, even conclusive. As if the knot of his existential dilemma were about to come undone.

The meeting with Antonio, the dancer, never took place. Ceferino forgot to go see him. He lost all notion of reality, and with it, he forgot the reasons for his trip entirely. His eyes and his will belonged only to that goddess, the rest of his responsibilities be damned. The last heat of summer was still in the air during those weeks he spent with her, and when September came to an end, he had to return to the United States to prepare for war. He had made it out of Spain unharmed, that much he knew. But he wasn't so sure he would be able to avoid Korea.

The police stopped him almost as soon as he set foot in America. León was just a kid, he didn't have the heart to be a soldier, and he was about to face a military tribunal that would judge him for—who knew?—sedition, desertion, high treason. It was serious, the US was embarking upon a war, and he had turned his back on the country that had taken him in and given him an identity.

They shut him up in the brig on the base in Sacramento. He didn't know how long he would be in that hellhole, but there was one thing he had faith in: despite everything, he was still lucky. Two long, monotonous days and nights passed, enough for him to reflect on what he'd been through since he'd left his home in Barcelona three years ago.

On the afternoon of the third day, they came to fetch him.

"Lion, come out of your cage!" The warden was making fun of his name.

"What is it? Where to now?" León asked, disconcerted, emerging from his cell.

"This is your first inspection," the soldier told him. "It doesn't look good for you, León."

They walked to the sergeant's office, where the door was cracked open. The soldier knocked, then stood at attention and brought his hand up to his temple as he announced to his superior:

"Sir, Justo Ramón León, sir."

"Come in!" a deep voice commanded from inside.

For the next week, Ceferino had to go through a series of interrogations, psychological tests, and physical exams that left him exhausted but unbroken. After a few more days in his cell with no further interruptions, the surly soldier who watched over him constantly opened the door and handed him a piece of paper, telling him to get his things and go: "There's no room here for traitors to their country." The document Justo León held in his hands was his passport to freedom. The medical committee in charge of León's file had declared him *Unfit for military service*.

Ceferino left the base and headed straight for the bus station. On the ten-hour ride to Los Angeles, he had time to think about what he would do. He had decided to stop giving in to that maddening despair that had dogged him during the past year, holding him back, crushing his initiative. He was tired of taking baby steps. He wanted to jump in with both feet. To put it all on the line.

A brave person does things his own way, he told himself. *Nobody's deciding for me,* he resolved, remembering his father's words. And he made a choice. First of all, he was going to be someone. New. Reinvented. He had thought of a name, a real one. One he would keep forever. He said goodbye, once and for all, to Justo Ramón León, not to mention Ceferino Carrión.

He was ready to pounce. Like that lion in the imposing and majestic Roman Colosseum he had admired in a painting in Paris during the impasse between his flight from Barcelona and his departure from Le Havre.

When Cefe and his fellow exiles, Pedro and Jaime, had arrived in that beautiful city, they'd moved into the attic of a Spaniard who had taken them in after seeing them wandering around Notre-Dame. Paris was about to celebrate the fifth year of its liberation from the Nazis, and the city was getting its groove back, swaying to the rhythms of jazz and swing, music the Americans had left behind. While Cefe and his friends worked in dive bars in the Latin Quarter, Ceferino absorbed the nightlife in a free city where art and culture were flourishing wherever you turned. At one of the many exhibits he saw, Ceferino was captivated by the works of one particular artist. Above all, he couldn't stop looking at one painting showing a lion waiting respectfully while the martyrs prayed to God one last time. A final goodbye.

The painter was Jean-Léon Gérôme, and Ceferino decided on this name from that moment forward: Jean Leon.

And now he was ready at last: *Growl you may, but go you must.*

CHAPTER 4

As soon as Jean Leon settled into his new life in Los Angeles, he devoted himself, sometimes obsessively, to impersonation. He observed, compared, imitated, and reproduced behaviors and expressions he had thought would never come naturally to him. He brought the same steadfast ambition to his ever-impeccable manner of dress: jacket and tie, to give him style and elegance, to conceal his still-gawky body, and to add a touch of seriousness to his baby face. Jean Leon had an idol— he wanted to look like him, be like him, make it as far as he had. Jean Leon adopted his dress and mannerisms, tried to imitate his imperturbable poise: Frank Sinatra, the coolest of the cool.

The first time Jean had encountered the star was on his date with Eva María. They watched, hand in hand, as Sinatra, in a sailor's uniform, sang "New York, New York" on the streets of the big city with Gene Kelly and Jules Munshin. Coming out of the theater, Jean had told his cousin Julio, Lara, and Eva María that his dream was to be an actor. It comforted him that Sinatra was lanky like him, and that gave him hope that he, too, could make it as an actor.

It was April 1953. Three years had passed since he'd been declared unfit for the military and had said goodbye to the name Ceferino Carrión. He was Jean Leon now. On life's horizon lay a long line of promises and dreams yet to be conquered.

Jean eventually got a job working for Hollywood Yellow Cabs, driving a taxi on the night shift. It wasn't his dream job, but he knew his time would come. The zone he was assigned to included Hollywood, but he had never come across anyone famous. Until one fateful night when the dispatcher sent him to Capitol Records, and the taxi door opened. In climbed a beautiful woman followed by the idol himself, Frank Sinatra.

"To Villa Capri!" the singer ordered sternly.

Sinatra took off his black felt hat with its narrow brim and white ribbon, a stylish contrast with his discreet striped suit and thin black tie. The woman wore a champagne-colored dress and didn't take off her sunglasses. She removed a gold-filtered cigarette from the handbag resting on her knees and lit up. It was Ava Gardner.

"Right away!" Leon responded agreeably.

He wanted to make a good impression and keep it professional, but as soon as he pulled out, his nerves got the best of him and the car bucked, making the couple lurch forward. They didn't seem to notice, though—they were arguing, and stayed at it the whole way to the restaurant. Leon was on edge, but he hid it, keeping his eyes pinned to the road. He pretended not to hear a word, but it was impossible not to eavesdrop on their dispute.

"We're not having it, Frank," Ava Gardner said curtly, exhaling a cloud of smoke.

"What do you mean we're not having it?" Sinatra asked. He, too, had lit a cigarette.

"You know good and well what I mean. Our relationship is a goddamn roller coaster. We can barely take care of ourselves, and you want us to have a baby?"

The actress's voice was cold and penetrating.

"Plus, the studio will fire me," she said.

"You should never have signed that contract."

"Like I had a choice," she said sarcastically. "It's not the first time I've had to get an abortion. Or do you not know how these things work?"

"Isn't it mine?" Sinatra butted in, apparently worried.

"Who else's would it be?"

It was hard to tell if the woman's insensitivity came from indifference or resignation. But it was obvious her words hurt Sinatra.

"I'm not about to bring a baby into the world so it can suffer through this mess," Gardner said, shielded by her glasses, which allowed her to avoid ever looking at her companion.

"So my opinion doesn't count for anything?"

Sinatra stared gloomily at his reflection in the glasses. It was clear he wouldn't find a happy resolution to their argument. She was holding the reins. Ava Gardner, who had made him fly to the moon, as he had sung in that song written by Bart Howard, was now throwing him back down to earth. Leon would find out eventually just how head over heels Sinatra was for this woman, how crazy she made him.

Leon could appreciate Sinatra's dilemma, to some extent. He, too, always found himself drawn to girls who were wild and unmanageable—or who tried to get him into a long-term relationship. He had always refused to be tied down. But then, he had never been with a woman as captivating and self-assured as Gardner. He visualized the kind of woman he'd like to have by his side, the kind of woman who could bewitch him the way Ava Gardner had bewitched Sinatra.

"Look at us, Frank!" Gardner continued her raging. "Our career is our life, and not even that is stable. We can't have kids."

"I have three, and—"

"And what? And what?" Ava seemed ready to go for the throat. "Three kids you've abandoned, and their mother to boot! That's what you call being a father? Come on, Frank! Who are we trying to fool? Having children is for regular people, not for us."

Jean Leon pulled to a stop in front of Villa Capri, and the couple fell silent, bringing their discussion to a temporary close—though it was clearly far from over.

"Here we are," Leon dared to utter, his voice faint, his eyes glued to the steering wheel.

Gardner didn't wait for Frank but strode quickly into Villa Capri alone. The singer handed Leon a twenty-dollar bill and got out of the taxi in a rage, slamming the door behind him and disappearing into the restaurant. Later that night, when Leon returned his taxi to the depot, he noticed Sinatra had left a tape in the back seat. Leon, of all people, knew an opportunity when he saw one.

The next day, Leon entered the exclusive Villa Capri for the first time, looking around in wonder. The place was well known to all as a magnet for stars and the press. All the aspiring actors jockeyed to get a table there: it was *the* place to see and be seen. It was spacious and divided into two distinct areas: On one side was the lounge, with walls of exposed stone and wood and a padded bar the customers on their barstools would lean on while they drank. On the other side, in the dining room, the tables were arranged so guests could hear the music from the piano next to the cigarette machine.

The place was empty at that hour. Jean Leon was disappointed—he would have loved to sit and people-watch for hours.

"You're looking for Mr. Sinatra?" The question, asked by a man emerging from the back of the restaurant, unsettled him.

"Yesterday I brought him here in a taxi, and he left this." He showed the man the tape.

The other man's attitude changed, and he reached out for Leon to hand it to him.

"I'm sure Mr. Sinatra will want to show you his gratitude. If you wouldn't mind leaving me a way to get in touch with you . . ."

Jean Leon passed him a card with the taxi company's number and his name, but he insisted on handing the tape to the singer himself. The maître d' looked at him disdainfully.

"What, you don't trust me?"

"No, sir, it's not that . . . You understand," he said softly.

The maître d' looked him over again from head to toe and disappeared, grumbling some curt comment about miserable bastards who'll do anything for a tip. After a few seconds, Sinatra himself appeared in the door between the kitchen and the dining room. He waved the taxi driver over and sat down with him at a table near the bar.

Sinatra thanked him effusively for returning something so valuable to him. The tape contained all the recordings of the songs for his new album. After asking Leon how much money he made as a taxi driver, Sinatra offered him a job as a waiter in the restaurant.

While the two talked, a half dozen people came over to Sinatra's table. They greeted him, nodding and squeezing his hand, made witty remarks, or praised him with what seemed like sincerity. Leon had the feeling he was watching some kind of ritual. And these repeated shows of respect intoxicated him. Leon knew the finer points of all these interactions were lost on him, but still, he finally had a chance to observe Sinatra in his element. He'd been waiting for something like this to happen for years.

Just a few minutes in the presence of the superstar offered Leon his first chance to get a sense of the composure, the presence you needed if you were going to become something in that city—which was like a stage, where appearances and illusions were everything. His meeting with Sinatra had lasted just a few moments, but it had changed everything for Leon. And he knew how to make something of this opportunity. Soon enough, he wouldn't be just a former taxi driver to whom Sinatra owed a small favor. He would be a trusted confidant.

Just over a year and a half later, at one in the morning on November 5, 1954, Sinatra showed up at Villa Capri straight from Capitol Records, just a few blocks from the restaurant. Whenever he was in LA recording or doing shows, he usually dined there, stretching the night out as long as he could. He never came alone. That night, his companion was his friend and manager Hank Sanicola. Jean Leon led them to the singer's usual table and served them dinner. The night passed calmly until, during dessert, an enraged Joe DiMaggio ran into the restaurant and headed straight for Sinatra's table.

"That slut! That goddamn whore!"

Behind the baseball star, who was a partner in some of Sinatra's businesses, was Barney Ruditsky, a private detective on DiMaggio's payroll. Not even a month ago, Marilyn Monroe had filed for divorce from DiMaggio, and he couldn't stand the thought that in that short time, she'd already replaced him. The list of candidates was unnerving: at the top of the list were the actor Robert Mitchum and the musician Hal Schaefer. Then there was a notorious lesbian he only knew by her first name: Sheila.

"Sit down, Joe, relax!" Sinatra said, meeting eyes with Leon over by the bar.

"She can't even wait for the divorce?" DiMaggio roared in frustration.

"Don't let that stuff go to your head," Frank said, trying to calm his friend down.

"Ruditsky," DiMaggio said, pointing at the detective, "has a very reliable source who says Marilyn's with her lover right now."

"Now? Where are they?"

"In some apartments over on Waring," Ruditsky butted in. "I told Joe I can go over right now, snap a few photos, and she'll be up a creek when we go to court."

"That ain't good enough," the athlete said, draining the drink Leon had served him.

Sinatra, DiMaggio, and Sanicola jumped up from the table. Ruditsky followed suit. The four of them, Jean learned later, got in the manager's car and headed toward the apartments on Waring. It was a short drive, no more than five minutes at that late hour. They wanted to surprise Marilyn in the act. All they had to do was find the apartment—the one that faced the street, according to Ruditsky's information. They got out in silence and walked toward the unlit entrance. They stood on both sides of the door. When no one opened up, DiMaggio took the bull by the horns and kicked the door down in a rage.

They went in ready to teach the lovers a lesson, and DiMaggio started first, pounding on one of the two people in the bed.

"It's not her, it's not her!" screamed Ruditsky, watching the girl jump out of bed and run off to hide in the bathroom. She was brunette, with long hair, and didn't look a damn thing like Marilyn.

Meanwhile, an enraged Joe DiMaggio kept unloading his fury and frustration on his wife's supposed lover, a chunky, bald guy who absorbed half a dozen punches from one of the strongest arms in the big league. The outfielder milked the moment for all he could, dealing out blows that could have torn a tree up by its roots.

When Sinatra realized their mistake, he ordered everyone to leave. "Let's get out of here!"

They had to drag out DiMaggio, who was blind with rage at the supposed adultery. Ruditsky was at a loss.

"I don't know what happened . . ."

"Can it!" said Sinatra. "I don't want to hear another word come out of your fucking mouth, otherwise I'll sew it shut for you, got that?" The Voice was shooting fire out of his eyes.

They hurried back to Villa Capri. It was two in the morning and there wasn't a soul on the road. Only two waiters were left in the restaurant. One of them was Jean Leon.

"What happened?" Leon dared to ask from behind the bar, where he was cleaning up when they barged back in.

Sinatra had an innate sense of whether or not he could trust a person. And he decided to confess what had happened.

"If anyone asks, we've been here all night, understand?" he said, confident the staff would take his side.

Soon enough, the police burst into Villa Capri, looking for anyone involved in an assault on a couple. The two people had reported four assailants—the very number of guests seated at the table where the police now stood. The bruised victim, standing between the officers, identified two of them right away. Sinatra and Joe DiMaggio were too well known to go unnoticed.

"Inspector," Sinatra began in a conciliatory tone, "we're a couple of good old friends who met here for a bite to eat, and as you can see, we were just headed out. Isn't that right, boys?"

They all lied. The waiter and bartender, too, when the detectives questioned them. Leon took the initiative, and his account was apparently convincing. They still said he'd have to testify in court—but the trial wouldn't start for quite some time, and since the accused had two witnesses speaking on their behalf while the accusers had none, the charge was eventually thrown out.

Thanks to that episode, Sinatra started taking special care of Jean Leon. Every night, he gave him a hundred-dollar tip, and Leon knew that he was now part of Sinatra's inner circle. He was one of his guys, and that was something very few people could say.

CHAPTER 5

"Hey, Jimmy, what are you doing here all by yourself?"

For days, Jean Leon had noticed his friend James Dean was quieter, more distracted, than usual.

"I don't feel up to it tonight."

"Everyone's here, though."

"Exactly."

Mrs. Schneider's acting school, a place many of the most renowned Hollywood faces of the day had passed through, was just next door to Villa Capri. It was a time of major social, political, and artistic upheaval, and of major productions and vitality in the cinema industry. There was talent wherever you looked, especially among a new wave of actors and actresses trained in the schools that followed the lead of the pioneering Actors Studio, founded by Elia Kazan a few years before in New York. For a while, even Jean Leon had tried the Stanislavsky method, a system developed by Konstantin Stanislavsky in the USSR and adopted by the Actors Studio in 1947, but it didn't work for him: he couldn't get into his characters' shoes the way his friends could, and he wasn't very striking physically. With a measure of frustration—which he kept closely guarded—he decided to focus his energies on other projects that were whirling around in his head. And so he put an end to his short-lived dream of becoming an actor, but he refused to leave behind that world that so enthralled him.

His close contact with the acting students led to important friendships, especially with the people who hung out in Sinatra's restaurant after class. They were a group of kids who had managed to shed the stigma of "wannabes," though they weren't yet stars, either. New faces not afraid to mingle with Hollywood legends. They had taken their first steps in the cinema world, and they liked hanging out together. Jean Leon hit it off with a quartet of rebels without a cause: Natalie Wood, a child actor who longed to be taken seriously; Sal Mineo; Dennis Hopper; and Jimmy Dean. Later on, Warren Beatty, Robert Wagner, and Paul Newman would join the group, though they never became core members. As would Pier Angeli, born Anna Maria Pierangeli, who had bewitched James Dean years before and was sitting with the group that night in the restaurant.

"I'm out of here," Jimmy said, playing with his Zippo. "You want to join me?"

When he was nervous or upset, Jimmy would fixate on some object to fiddle with—often, that old lighter his father had given him when he came back from the war. *We were on our way to the bowling alley in his Chevrolet,* he'd explained to Jean once, *and I remember what he told me when he gave it to me: the flame won't go out even if you're on a motorcycle. The way it's made, with a hinged top, makes it very hard to put out. You can't blow on it, you can't shake it. It only goes out when you close the lid.*

"My shift's not over yet."

Dean shook his head. Leon, who knew him only too well, could see how agitated he was. He knew Dean wouldn't get out of that spiral until he gave his thoughts free rein.

"What is it, Jimmy?"

"Anna Maria's family doesn't want us to be together."

"What do you mean?"

"Her mother's found a better husband for her. They already got a wedding date."

A better husband? Jean thought, still looking at his friend with worry. "What's her mother got against you?"

"Who knows!" Dean exclaimed, indignant. "She doesn't want a guy like me for her daughter, a guy who only thinks about cars and motorcycles."

What a hypocrite, Jean thought with distaste. If only Anna Maria's mother could see the positive influence that her daughter had on his friend, and how she was growing beside him. The girl's soft, delicate manner was like a salve for Dean's wild spirit; she tamed his most rebellious instincts. They complemented each other perfectly.

"I love her," he whispered, head lowered, eyes closed.

And with a characteristic click, James closed the lid of the Zippo. He took a few intense drags of his cigarette, pinching it between his thumb and forefinger and sucking down as much as he could of the blond tobacco that calmed his nerves. He blew out the smoke softly, threw the butt to the floor, and ground it out with his heel.

"You'll find another one who won't just give in to her parents," Jean said, trying to encourage his friend.

"That's easy for you to say. You've got Donna."

Donna. It was true. Jean had fallen head over heels in love recently, and Jimmy had watched the whole thing from up close.

It all started with a pre-shift meal at a nearby restaurant called the Brown Derby, a casual joint not far from Villa Capri. It was the furthest thing imaginable from a restaurant in the old country: shaped like an enormous hat, with red flower beds lining the brim, it was a draw for Los Angeles big shots. There was a liquor store inside, and if his tips had been good one week, Leon would leave with a bottle of Burgundy or Bordeaux. He'd been going there more and more lately, and it looked like he would soon become a regular: his server that day, a girl with long blond hair and a bright smile, bewitched him from the first moment she approached his table.

"Jean?" she asked him.

"Yes, Jean Leon."

He leaned back into his studded leather booth, glancing nervously at the framed head shots of famous customers lining the walls, then met eyes with her. And once he had, he couldn't look away.

"Your name has so much personality to it. Are you French?" Donna asked.

"Yep, from old Europe. And you—are you new here?"

"Yeah, today's my first day," she said, a bit abashed. "You'll have to be a little patient."

"I've got all the patience in the world . . ." Jean looked at her name tag. "Donna."

"All the patience in the world, huh?" the girl repeated, intrigued by the customer in his spotless, uncreased uniform. He was a nice young man with a sweet face but a slightly reserved stare and seductive, drooping eyelids. He looked at once gentle and dangerous.

When he'd paid and said goodbye to her with a barely suppressed timidity, she told him later, she'd hoped to see him again. He wasn't like the loners she had waited on in other places, who would lean on the bar hoping to get something more than just attention. She finished her first shift at the restaurant with the feeling that after a year in Hollywood, as far as could be from her hometown, the one she'd been desperate to leave, something good was finally about to happen to her.

And something good did. For some time now, Donna's best friend, Connie Buchanan, had been berating her, saying, *A girl as pretty as you, and a good person to boot, shouldn't be alone*—and only a week had passed since she'd gone from *You should have a boyfriend* to *We've found the perfect person for you. He's a friend of my husband's, he's a good guy.* Before she had time to react, Donna had been wrangled into a blind date. At the very least, she wanted it to be on her home turf, so she suggested the restaurant where she worked, and that night at the Brown Derby, they sat at the same table where Clark Gable had proposed to Carole Lombard.

"It's a sign!" Connie said roguishly, winking at her friend.

Donna could never have imagined the date her best friend had set her up with would be that gawky, exotic young man who always came in to eat during her shift. She was delighted. Now, finally, she'd get to know more than just his name: Jean Leon.

"It is a sign!" Donna agreed.

After the obligatory formalities, still surprised at his luck, Jean asked her, "Jefferson City? Where's that?" The woman seated across from him was beautiful, and every word she uttered intrigued him.

"In Missouri."

"So what's a girl like you doing so far from home?" His voice betrayed his poorly concealed nerves.

"What's a boy like you doing even farther from home?"

The knowledge that both of them had pulled up roots and run off to Hollywood to start a new life brought them closer. They felt relieved, and somehow less alone in that overwhelming city.

Soul mates? They didn't want to get ahead of themselves.

"I left without my parents' blessing," Donna told him.

"Really?"

"Vera, my older sister, had already come to live in LA, and my parents didn't want to lose their younger daughter, too. Especially not for what they thought was a completely ridiculous dream."

"What dream is that?"

"Being an actress. Not very original."

"That makes two of us," he said. The coincidence amused them. "But the truth is, I'm less and less sure about the acting thing."

"I haven't had much luck so far," she conceded. "A half dozen castings in a year. But you know what? I'm not giving up."

"The world belongs to the brave."

Leon raised an imaginary glass of wine in support. Donna was flustered. The waiter came over to take their order, and Donna grabbed the reins.

"A Cobb salad for the gentleman."

It was Jean's favorite dish, one he always ordered. That salad was a classic at the Brown Derby. It was a simple dish, with all the ingredients chopped: lettuce, tomato, crispy bacon, chicken breast, hard-boiled egg, avocado, blue cheese, onions, and a special vinaigrette. Donna ordered one, too. Despite having worked there for weeks, she had still never tried the salad. It seemed they shared the same taste in food as well.

Soul mates?

In the background, a song was playing: "That's Amore," by Dean Martin, and it made them fall silent. *Is this another sign?* Donna wondered. They looked each other intensely in the eyes, and he took her hand.

After that first date came others. Things moved fast, and when the time came, Donna said "Yes" very softly, gently biting his lip just afterward. For more than a year, the entire time she'd lived in the city, she had turned down offers for hollow flings, preferring to keep herself for something better. Jean respected her chastity, but soon, kisses, caresses, and heated words were no longer enough for him. In the heat of passion, they took off for Las Vegas, more than two hundred miles away, stopping to spend the night in a roadside motel in a town with a prophetic name—Paradise.

Once they had gotten the keys to the only room they could afford, they walked, holding hands, across the parking lot toward their humble suite. Inside, they left the suitcase on the floor, closed the door brusquely behind them, and embraced, sharing a long, intense kiss. Their impatient fingers hurriedly pulled, unbuttoned, and tore at their clothing.

After they'd made love for the first time, on top of the stiff, starched sheets, Jean smoked and toyed with one of Donna's curls, which had fallen over her chest. As he caressed her, he couldn't help but let his fingers descend, sliding over her body, covered in pearls of sweat. Again, Donna arched her back when she felt his soft touch, and a gentle moaning accompanied her movement. They made love for a second time, more slowly. Without hurrying, without any demands, without holding back.

She lit another cigarette. She sat up partway and offered it to her husband-to-be, who sat leaning against the headboard.

"I like everything about you," Jean said. "Your blond hair, those honey-brown eyes, your beautiful lips, that little dimple in your chin, it drives me wild. I feel like I'm living in a dream, but I see you, and it's real. Do you love me, Donna?"

She kissed him on the corner of the lips. "Yes," she murmured. The next day, she repeated that *yes* in the wedding chapel. "Yes," she said, clearly, with feeling, as Jean slid on the simple ring they had chosen just minutes before asking for their marriage license.

They were young, they were in love, and they had just married. They both felt they were living in a dream, and neither wanted to wake up. *This is a sign!* They felt lucky—invincible, even. And so, that night, they bet everything they had in the casino. And they won. They won big.

The money from Las Vegas was enough to make a down payment on their first home. To start a life together, a life where they could make their dreams reality. Not only their individual dreams, but their dreams as a couple, as a family. But sometimes, two people's dreams aren't the same.

CHAPTER 6

"Why don't you go inside and get a pizza? It'll do you good. You can think better on a full stomach," Leon encouraged a grumpy James Dean. "Plus, now you're making enough to pay for a whole one yourself."

Jimmy laughed.

A year earlier, when the group of actors had started frequenting Villa Capri, it wasn't so much to eat—they couldn't afford anything on the menu—as to see and be seen. But then, that was why everyone was there. All of them were short on cash, and the most they could aspire to was splitting a pizza five or six ways. Jean Leon used to give them one or sometimes two extra for free, always making sure the boss, Billy Kant, a frustrated actor himself, didn't find out. As those young prodigies devoured their food, Jean watched them go over their scripts one last time before auditions and callbacks. Whenever they landed a role, he congratulated them.

Jimmy was Jean's best friend in the group, and they were growing closer by the day. Their relationship was cemented one day when he found Dean lost in thought, in a melancholy mood he would soon understand was a basic part of the actor's character. Dean was sociable, but only to a point. Whoever knew and loved him would respect his occasional need to flee the company of others. *Imagine you were at a party no one invited you to,* he told Jean once, *that's what it feels like for me sometimes, and I just don't know how to play along.* Dean made an exception for him, and often shared his secrets with Jean even when he had pulled away from everyone else.

They recognized each other as dreamers—people who dreamed with their eyes open—and knew they could share not only their plans and longings but also their sorrows and disappointments with each other.

They had similar temperaments: curiosity about the world, a permanent state of alertness, an unwillingness to give in easily. This was the first time in his North American adventure that Jean Leon found a true friend, a soul mate. They spoke the same emotional language and they listened to each other attentively.

They didn't always see eye to eye. But Jimmy never tried to impose his will, and that made him a person you could turn to. Jean, Jimmy knew, was looking for the kind of security that came from having a family, a home, and his own business—just the things Jimmy had fled from in boredom: for him, life was supposed to be about adventure and danger. Leon looked toward the future while Dean tried to wring every drop out of the present, living as hard as he could in the moment, as if death were eternally around the corner. But they understood each other. Something in Dean's introverted, impassioned character clicked with Leon in the deepest part of himself.

They found lots of common ground in their pasts. Both had left home, pulled up roots, and maintained no contact with their families. They treated each other as brothers and confidants.

Dean was from Indiana, Leon from Spain, and each wanted to make his name in Hollywood, albeit through different paths. They were both young, and both were as far as could be from the conservative conformism of the time. Both had rigged things to get out of fighting in Korea. And both had suffered through losing a parent at a very early age: Jimmy's mother died when he was nine years old, and at thirteen,

Leon had seen his father and brother disappear. Those losses marked them forever.

Jimmy liked hearing stories about the Carrión children. He imagined a house full of boys and girls of all ages peeking in and out of the doors and windows like in a vaudeville show. Jean laughed at the comparison. When he told those stories, he got back a part of his old self—Ceferino, the boy he'd decided to keep hidden to protect himself in America. Those conversations also helped him deal with the memory of José, his older brother.

"You miss him?"

"A lot. José was my hero."

Jean thought about José often. He had always looked up to his brother, and now he missed him. He would have liked to have José there, to ask him for advice, to learn from him, to grow up by his side. He would have introduced him to Jimmy. Jean knew the three of them would have been good friends. Would José have been proud of how far Jean had made it on his own?

"He saved my life. I was just a kid, it was Corpus Christi, we were all excited for the celebrations . . . When the sun came up, a group of us kids from Sant Martí went off into the woods, with my brother in the lead. My mother tried to get me to stay home, but José convinced her. We wanted to leave before it was too bright out to gather broom and boxwood, and get back in time to make the flower carpets for the procession. I loved that holiday so much . . . The streets were filled with flowers and colors and such intense fragrances. The carpets are like works of art on the ground—they're made of flower petals, seeds, all kinds of stuff unique to our region. And the scent—you can't believe how good it smells. Families used to open their balconies to let a little ray of life into their homes.

"We wanted to make sure the parade would walk over the carpet on our street. It had to be the best-smelling, best-decorated one in the neighborhood. We needed flowers from the other side of a hanging bridge that traversed a fast-running stream, where the water crashed against the rocks. It was a gravity-defying structure made of reeds, so it bent with the wind but wouldn't break. It was as safe as it was tough—it had been through lots of storms with pounding winds, and only ever came close to breaking during an earthquake. You had to cross it a few people at a time, in single file, holding on to the sides to keep the bridge from bouncing. No one dared to say it aloud, but everyone was scared of losing their balance and falling—or even worse, of the bridge breaking and the currents carrying us away.

"We all had our baskets tied to our backs and we walked across, one by one. I was the second to last, with José behind me. I clutched the sides and walked forward with a sure step, even though my legs were growing weak. The boards creaked beneath my feet. I prayed to every saint I could think of, and I only relaxed when I was across. Just around the curve, we saw spectacular waterfalls. At that point, the flow of the water slowed and wasn't so ferocious. I was entranced, watching how it wound among the rocks and dropped down into a tranquil little brook.

"We were almost to the place where we would gather the flowers when I slipped over the mossy rocks on a stretch of damp, swampy earth, lost my balance, and fell into a deep black pool of water, reaching for my brother's arm as I did. José knew how treacherous that area was—the falling water formed a whirlpool that could easily pull you down into the depths and kill you. But there was no time to be afraid. He would do anything possible to dig me out of that watery grave.

"*Cefe!*' José shouted. *'Cefe!*"

Realizing he'd revealed his old name, Leon corrected himself quickly: "That was what they used to call me back then."

"Following an instinct that was little more than a reflex," Leon continued, "he threw me a rope to grab on to. But it was too late. He couldn't see anything, not a single movement. The water was dark and worrisomely calm, no bubbles rising to the surface, as if it had just swallowed me up. The entire group panicked. José prayed I would pop up somewhere else downstream. After a brief silence that José told me seemed like an eternity, they saw a few first bubbles rise up and José could feel a slight pulling on the rope. Then he saw my hand coming up out of the water, grasping the rope.

"My brother shouted, *'Help me, come on, help! We've got to get him out of there!'* They all obeyed and got behind José to pull with all their strength on that rope, which was wet now, and heavier than before. My body emerged from the water of the tide pool. First one arm, then my torso, and finally my legs. *'You were deadweight,'* my brother told me a little later. I had been completely unconscious, but—and I still don't know how—I grabbed that rope in a final reflex before passing out.

"They managed to pull me up. They had a hell of a time getting me to start breathing and come to again. All I remember was the way I shook from the cold. I don't know how long it took me to recover. We decided we wouldn't say anything back home, and we returned at midday, later than we had planned, with our baskets full of flowers.

"I get goose bumps whenever I remember it. If my brother had given up on me, I wouldn't be here now. I think that's why I don't like to give up or let myself be beaten."

"You'll see," Jimmy said. "Someday you'll be able to visit your family again."

A jab of longing pierced Jean when he talked about them, and Jimmy could sense it. He knew Jean was on the run from the Spanish military, that he couldn't even contact them for fear of reprisal. *Maybe someday,* Jean agreed silently, shaking off his sorrow. He still had a lot of reasons to be happy.

Dean's presence helped Jean get over his mixed feelings about his past and grasp the possibilities the future offered him.

James Dean's vitality was contagious. By his side, Jean Leon felt anything could happen. Anything.

Even a restaurant of his own.

The idea had begun with an innocuous conversation one evening. Dean told him that when he had arrived in Santa Monica, years earlier, he had felt instantly at ease, even though it was a random event that had brought him there from Indiana. The Los Angeles VA hospital had offered Jimmy's father a job as a dental technician and had set him up with a house in the area. A bungalow next to the beach, in Pacific Palisades. After his mother died, Jimmy had to go back to Indiana, but he'd returned to California as soon as he could. He felt at home there, and he was thinking of setting down roots. Jean Leon's mind raced ahead of him. He, too, wanted permanence, a place he could call his own. But not a home. Something more, something his hopes could latch onto.

"If what you've got in mind is a restaurant, you can count me in," Jean told Jimmy.

The comment, uttered off the cuff, left a mark on both of them. The idea stuck in their minds, and they started thinking and planning in earnest. The money question was ironed out first. Dean had made $20,000 for *East of Eden*. His performance won him accolades, and the actor had now begun his transformation into an authentic phenomenon. They soon paid him $50,000 for *Rebel Without a Cause*. And before he knew it, he was signing a contract for *Giant*, his next film, worth $100,000. Only twenty-four years old, and people were calling him the new Marlon Brando. Just like Marlon, he shuffled his feet, turned round suddenly, gesticulated wildly, mumbled, swallowed his words, leaned against the wall.

The actor agreed to put up money for the restaurant, which they would design together, little by little. The dream was slowly becoming a reality. Dean and Leon met whenever they could at a corner table in the back of Villa Capri. They worked out numbers on napkins and sketched rough designs of the space that would become their restaurant. A prominent bar, with lush booths reserved for the stars and large tables with ample space between them—protecting their guests from curious gawkers. They would serve practical, simple dishes, familiar but elegant and sophisticated: *We need to offer a quality service suited to our clientele,* they both agreed. They were anxious, at times overwhelmed, but most of all excited.

One morning in April, Leon made an agreeable discovery. He was on his way to work when, out of the corner of his eye, he saw a "For Rent" sign in the window of La Scala in Beverly Hills. Despite the Italian name, the guy in charge of the restaurant was a Galician from La Coruña in Spain named José Amor—Americanized as Joe Amor. His place had never lost its Galician feel, even if the menu offered hamburgers and spaghetti alongside empanadas and *caldeiradas*. Jean Leon went there with Donna once or twice a month, because the seafood in garlic sauce was like a little vacation in Galicia. When they ate there, he felt close to the city of Santander, where he was born, and these little culinary journeys filled Jean with a joyful energy rather than bittersweet nostalgia.

Jean Leon went in and found Joe Amor at one of the tables, going over a pile of invoices. With one hand, he was adding up columns of numbers, and with the other, he held a pair of reading glasses in front of his eyes.

"Hey, Jean," Joe said, warm as ever, smiling and offering him a seat.

"What's going on with the sign? You leaving the business?"

"I'm giving it up, son, retiring. I'll hang up my apron this summer. I can't do it anymore! You know how it is." Jean nodded knowingly. "This line of work demands patience and energy, and I'm starting to run out of both."

"I'll never find another place with cooking like yours," Jean complained.

"You're wrong there. Emilio's sticking around."

Joe's nephew, Emilio Nuñez, was the chef there, and an immensely talented one, from Jean's point of view. He was the one who had authored the menu, the unique fusion of several different traditions that was the restaurant's hallmark. At just twenty-four years old, Emilio had chalked up more hours behind the oven than many veterans, and his dishes showed it. Joe Amor respected the kid's talent enough to make keeping him on a requirement for whoever bought the business. The idea struck Jean Leon—who was in his twenties himself—and he couldn't help but ask.

"How much are you asking for?"

"You really interested?" Amor asked, raising his eyebrows over his glasses.

"Well . . . It's something I've been thinking about a long time. Why not? I've even got a partner who's looking to get in the game. An actor, someone who's coming up in the world."

As Leon talked, he looked over the place with fresh eyes, remodeling it in his imagination. "It's a great spot, it's got a good chef. I'll be the maître d'. I know what I'm getting into. I don't want to just take care of the tables. I want it to be a restaurant where people will feel at home. Or better than at home. A place where, once they come, they'll want to keep coming back."

"Sounds like we can work something out."

The conversation stretched on, and more meetings followed, until the three men—Joe, Jean, and Emilio—finally reached an agreement. The restaurant would be Jean's in September. He had the cash, the cook, and the place. He was getting close.

Jimmy and Jean couldn't stop talking about it. Every time they saw each other, they would talk over their ideas, and when they got the chance, they would sit down to discuss the project with people they trusted, who could serve as a sounding board.

One Sunday evening, Jimmy had convinced an actor friend to accompany him to Villa Capri for a drink. Ronald Reagan was the host of *General Electric Theater*, the CBS network's star program, which brought millions of Americans together in front of the TV every week. The CBS building on Sunset Boulevard, where *General Electric Theater* was taped, was only a few blocks away from McCadden Place.

Reagan and Dean had met three times on the program already that year. The two men walked together over to Villa Capri, and Jean Leon greeted them at the front door.

Jimmy tapped the bottom of his pack of Lucky Strikes with his finger, and, as if by magic, three cigarettes emerged from the hole he had torn in the top. He offered one to Reagan, slipped another one between his lips, and pushed the third one back inside.

"What are you two up to at this hour? There's barely anyone still here!" Leon told them with a smile, spreading his arms out in the middle of the almost-empty restaurant. There was just one couple at a table—the actors Zsa Zsa Gabor and Tony Franciosa—and one guest at the bar, a screenwriter from MGM who was already waving for the check. "Come on in," a smiling Jean Leon said.

"I was just asking Ronnie what he thought about our idea," Jimmy told Leon.

"So?" Leon said, guiding them inside.

"It sounds like a smart move to me," Reagan said. "I've heard crazier things, that's for sure. Anyway, you can count me in as a customer."

"Why don't you sit down and chat with us for a while, Jean?" Dean proposed.

"Yeah, Jean, why not?" Reagan asked.

"Thanks, Jimmy, thanks, Ronnie," he said. "Maybe in a bit, when everybody's gone."

The actors walked off to an out-of-the-way table. In no time, Leon had the screenwriter out the door and got the check to Gabor and Franciosa, who paid quickly and left. It was a Sunday, after all, and even the stars have to go to work on Monday mornings. Leon walked them to the door and hung up the "Closed" sign.

His work more or less done—though he still had to count the drawer and clean up, so Capri would be immaculate for the morning shift—Leon decided to accept his friends' invitation for a drink. As he approached the table, he listened to the two men chatting.

"You know, I feel like this presenter role fits me better than acting," Ronnie said, sucking on a newly lit cigarette.

"I thought you were just doing it to make some coin while you waited on your agent to call," Dean said, surprised.

"I fired my agent. I'm a free man, totally free," Reagan said with a satisfied smile. "I like TV. I'd even say I love it. CBS gives me a window to peek out of every day and get inside the heads of everyone in America."

"Does this mean you're serious about getting into politics?"

Reagan's name had been ringing out as a possible addition to the Republican Party ever since he had left his post as president of the Screen Actors Guild for ideological reasons.

"Yeah, why not?" Reagan said. "I don't know how I feel about the way things are going. This is a great country, but maybe it's ready for a change. We need to get serious about the Soviets, about taxes, about everything!"

"You're looking riled up, there, Ronnie," Jean laughed as he refilled their glasses.

"Sit down, sit down, Jean," Dean said, shaking his hand. "Apparently our boy's not kidding when he says he might go into politics. I guess he didn't get enough when he was with the union . . ."

Reagan insisted the country's establishment needed new blood: "I just can't see Vice President Nixon taking over for Ike," he said. "He doesn't have the same determination or charisma. The Democrats are going to run someone young, this Kennedy guy, supposedly, this senator from Massachusetts. He's bright-eyed, an idealist, he's got a touch of Wilson to him, but I'm not sure if I like what he's selling. 'We respect the self-determination of peoples and free commerce,'" he declared sardonically. "With the way things are now, and the Soviets vying for world leadership!"

"Truth is, Ronnie, you already sound like a politician," Leon said.

"Listen, we're all doing politics! Even if we don't realize it," he said. "Our lives, our decisions, all that is politics—and if we don't take the lead, someone else will, and that could make things get ugly."

"You're telling me. Look at my country . . ."

Leon realized he had let something slip out that he shouldn't have. Few people knew he was Spanish; with his name, everyone assumed he was French, and he never bothered to correct the error. Jimmy was one of the few who was in on his secret. Now that the cat was halfway out of the bag, he told Reagan, too, and received a respectful nod in response.

"Franco's dictatorship has turned Spain upside down," Leon said. "Lots of people had to leave, like I did, to make their dreams come true, because there's no future there. You're right, Ronnie, with what you said about politics: if you can't choose for yourself, that means someone else is choosing for you."

"Enough about all that. I'd just as soon talk about our dreams for the future," Jimmy said, raising his glass and clinking the ice cubes inside.

"Damn right!" Leon raised his glass, too, then went even further. "First the restaurant, then who knows? Maybe even our own wine."

Leon's dreams were growing bigger and bigger. Jimmy and Ronnie looked at him askance and laughed.

"Hey, I picked grapes in France one time, and where I'm from, there's plenty of fertile land. You could grow the best wines in the world there," Leon explained with a grin. "Why not? Make a good wine we can serve in our own place. What do you say, Jimmy?"

Leon knew this was pushing it. But since he had started at Villa Capri, wine had become one of his passions. It had started with grateful regulars who would ask him to join them for a glass of Brunello or, if it was a special occasion, Château Lafite. He'd started paying attention, asking people what they drank and why, grilling the maître d's on what were the best bottles when he and Donna would go for a dinner out. He had seen the great names on the labels: Romanée-Conti, Pétrus, or, in California, Inglenook and Beaulieu. Why couldn't Jean Leon shine alongside them? As he and Dean always told each other, dreaming is free. And Reagan, who was listening to them as he swirled his drink, raised his glass and toasted to their castle in the sky.

"Sure thing, Jean! For you, a great wine; for Jimmy, a successful career. For both of you, a restaurant, and for me . . . heck, maybe I'll be president of the United States of America," he announced, sounding utterly convinced.

What he'd just blurted out surprised neither Dean nor Leon, but the alcohol they'd imbibed made them want to laugh anyway. Reagan raised his glass again and said to Jean Leon solemnly, as if giving an oath:

"And let me promise you something, Jean: when we make our dreams come true, we'll toast our successes with your wine."

They nodded and downed their glasses, and as the liquor warmed their insides, they looked at each other and laughed uproariously.

Of all the toasts that had been offered that night, it was those to James Dean's success that came true quickest, and that was a good omen for their future restaurant. But Dean's meteoric rise overwhelmed him, and he was often in a sour mood. He couldn't make peace with fame: acting was one thing, he was a careful and conscientious worker, but he wasn't ready to live under the microscope, let alone have to listen to constant praise—praise that, to his mind, anyway, always seemed slightly con-descending. He couldn't get comfortable under the halo of prestige and renown that the studios seemed bent on crowning him with. He first realized it one evening at Villa Capri. At the end of his meal, Dean reached back for his wallet, and Jean rested a hand on his shoulder.

"Times have changed, Jimmy. You can put things on your tab now."

"What are you talking about, Jean?"

"What I just said!" Dean looked surprised. "You can charge your meals here now, dummy." Billy Kant, the gruff manager of Villa Capri, had seen *East of Eden* at the Egyptian, and from that moment, he had started to treat James Dean like a VIP. As soon as Kant began to respect the group of young actors he couldn't stand just a few months before, James Dean decided he'd had enough.

"Listen, Jean, tell the manager to stick that tab up his ass!" Dean shook his head, his eyebrows rising over the black frames of his glasses, clearly angry. "If I wasn't good enough for a tab yesterday, I ain't good enough today, either. So I'll keep paying cash, and that's that!"

"Works just fine for me, Jimmy," Leon said calmly, chuckling to himself.

Dean took a long drag off the cigarette hanging from his lips and blew a few smoke rings.

"I'm tired of all this fakery. You want to know something? When I come back from filming in Texas, we gotta get to work. We're gonna make this restaurant happen. I'll take care of the money, and you take care of the rest."

"Jimmy . . ." Leon cleared his throat, feeling a knot in it that would barely let him speak.

They hugged, and before he said goodbye, Dean mumbled something Leon couldn't quite catch. It sounded like *Dream as if you'll live forever. Live as if you'll die today.*

If they were serious, truly serious about this—and they were—it was time for Jean Leon to do the one thing he dreaded most: tell Frank he was going to open his own restaurant. Sinatra notoriously prized loyalty above all else. How would he handle the news? Jean was petrified.

He spent days practicing, trying to figure out how to approach Sinatra. But try as he might, he was incapable of finding the right words, and he knew his friend wouldn't be happy about it.

"I have to tell him myself. He can't find out through someone else. He'd never forgive me, and we've got to have Frank on our side."

"Time's running out," Jimmy Dean said to him, aware that Jean was right. "You should tell him as soon as you can."

"It's got to be tonight."

But that night, Sinatra showed up at Capri more irritable than usual. He sat at his table alone—Jean had never seen him do that before. Jean hesitated, but only briefly. If he kept waiting for the right time, it would never come.

"Good evening, Frankie! Everything good?" Jean set down his usual, a glass of bourbon, a double. Frank didn't even need to ask. Jean brought the bottle with him; Sinatra wasn't a one-and-done type of guy.

Jean could read the Voice's mood from his stare, and that night it was glacial. It could be a new song he was recording that had set him off, a few extra scenes for his latest film, the headaches Ava Gardner gave him, or anything. Jean started to lose his nerve. But then he thought of what it would mean to stay on at that job, the same routine, day after day, always playing second fiddle . . . and that gave him the strength to speak up.

"When you've got a moment, we should talk," he said, determined to stop fretting.

There it is. All I've got to do is remember the words I practiced before.

"Whatever you say."

"Now, then? Well, what I want to tell you . . . It can wait till it's good for you. Say, after closing time."

"Stop beating around the bush. Sit down and tell me what you've got to say."

"Yes, sir. You're the boss." Jean took a seat beside him, shaken. He was drawing a blank.

Sinatra served himself another glass and downed it in one long sip. He did the same two more times, while Jean took deep breaths, trying to keep a grip on himself. He decided to just spit it out.

"I'm going to open . . . I mean, we're going to open a restaurant close to here. Right off of Santa Monica Boulevard."

"A restaurant? You and who else?"

"Jimmy Dean and me."

Sinatra smiled sardonically.

"You're going to go down in flames!"

"Why do you say that?"

"There's no room for another restaurant around here. All the good customers are already divvied up between Villa Capri, Romanoff's, and Chasen's."

"Yeah, but what we've got in mind is something different. Another type of cuisine, in a cozy environment."

"That's it?" Sinatra laughed contemptuously. "That's your recipe for your little restaurant's success?"

Jean Leon was having a hard time making his point, and he was starting to get frazzled. His voice trembled and he felt a cold sweat break out over his entire body.

"Oh, OK, now I get it!" shouted Sinatra. "You want my support. Probably you've already started trying to hoodwink our guests into going over to your place instead. I didn't expect that from you, Jean. Not from you."

"That's not it, Frank. If you'd let me explain . . ."

But Sinatra didn't want to hear another word.

Jean needed him to understand that this was a personal quest, an almost vital need. *I've got to fly on my own, Frankie,* he wanted to tell him. *I feel like my time has come, and I don't want to miss the boat.* Jean had gone to California looking for opportunities that had never come, but now, with the support of his friend James Dean, he was convinced he had his shot.

It wasn't the first time Jean had talked to Sinatra about the idea of having his own place. The singer had even offered to help him out. But Jean was never sure if he'd come through on the offer, and he couldn't imagine starting off as equals, not with all the ideas he had bubbling up in his head. Being Frank's associate for the rest of his life wasn't viable, but still, he was thankful for all he had learned from him, and he knew Frank's disapproval could sink him.

When the silence had stretched on too long, Jean Leon said goodbye. Sinatra took a big sip, trying to digest what he'd just heard, dried his lips with the back of his hand, and watched Leon as he walked away.

"Good luck to you."

From that night on, their relationship grew colder.

It took six years before they could patch things up. But despite his sadness over Frank's harsh words, Leon felt free. It wouldn't be long now.

The exterior filming of Dean's new film *Giant* lasted a month and a half down in Texas, and then Jimmy returned home for a few more weeks in the studio. On September 29, 1955, James Dean came to Villa Capri with some of his costars to celebrate the end of shooting. Liz Taylor and Rock Hudson were there, along with Sal Mineo and Carroll Baker. Dean was exultant. He was wearing white pants, a short-sleeved black polo, and a dark jacket. He held his pack of Lucky Strikes up to his mouth and pulled out the last one with his lips.

"I got good news, Jimmy," Jean said when he saw the actor come through the door.

"Me too. Sunday I'm racing in Salinas. I can't wait to put my new Spyder to the test!"

The actor's eyes were gleaming. He had signed a contract with the producer stating that he would stay away from the races while he was filming, but now he was off the leash.

"I'm happy for you," his friend said. "But remember, we've got a meeting at the bank on Monday. We need to sign the papers for the space, we gave them our word."

"Don't worry." Jimmy winked. "Ten on the dot. I'll be there. And relax, I won't make you watch my cat while I'm gone, I know you're allergic," he said, smiling.

"Damn right you won't!" shouted Leon, waving his hands around in a gesture of refusal.

"It's taken care of! Liz is helping me out," he said, amused, gesturing at the actress, who was chatting with Rock Hudson. "By the way, she told me to tell you she wants a chocolate martini."

Leon's relationship with Elizabeth Taylor, who was like a sister to Dean, had started with that particular cocktail at a party just before the start of filming for *Giant*.

"Give me a couple of chocolate martinis," the actress had asked Jean that night.

Leon was taken aback. He had never heard of such a thing. But he couldn't confess to her that he didn't know how to make one. She was Liz Taylor, for God's sake.

"Right away," he responded officiously. As he was looking around to see what ingredients he had on hand, Rock Hudson came over to her at the bar.

"Hey, Liz, what about my chocolate martini?" the actor asked.

"I was just about to bring it to you, Rock," she answered with a smile.

Leon quickly improvised, mixing vanilla extract, vodka, irish cream, and chocolate syrup, then finished it off with a dash of cocoa powder. He served them in martini glasses, one for each star. He didn't know what he was doing, but he had to risk it. The two stars toasted each other and took a sip. Taylor looked over at Jean. Nervous, he looked down, not wanting to meet her eyes and register her disappointment with him.

"You all right?" she asked him politely.

"Yeahhhh, why?" Leon asked.

"You don't look too hot," the actress said, staring at the bartender more closely, a frown playing on her face.

"It's great," Rock Hudson said, uninterested in Taylor's fretting, gulping the drink down in three seconds flat. "I told you! Give me another, please!" Leon recovered once he saw the actor had liked it. He swallowed with relief, and Taylor gave him a sly, astute glance.

"You never made a chocolate martini before, am I right?" she said in a soft voice, leaning in toward him.

Bewitched by Liz Taylor's famous eyes, Leon dropped his cover. He couldn't deceive her. He nodded curtly, and the actress burst out laughing.

"I'm not surprised. Rock and I just made it up!" she admitted. Leon turned bright red but chuckled gamely as he turned to prepare the second round.

The two actors started talking about James Dean. Leon kept his eyes down as he portioned out the first of the cocktails, listening to them spar back and forth over the bet that Hudson proposed.

"We'll see which one of us gets Dean into the sack first!"

"You don't have a chance, Rock! Just the other day he went with Cary Grant's ex," Taylor upbraided him.

"Who? Barbara Hutton?" Hudson asked, gesturing as if shooing flies away. "Whatever. If I win, will you give me what I ask for, Liz?"

"Whatever you wish, Rock!" Taylor responded, leaving her empty glass on the bar, winking at Leon, and taking Hudson's arm to return to the party.

By now Leon had memorized the measures and ingredients for the chocolate martini, and as he fixed Rock and Liz Taylor their drinks, he chatted with Jimmy, who came over and leaned on the bar.

"By the way, Jimmy, speaking of the race in Salinas . . . Isn't that where you filmed . . . ?"

"*East of Eden*. That's right. It's weird for me to be going back there. For me it wasn't a city, just a movie set," he said, looking up at the ceiling as he sipped his whiskey.

The next day, the photograph of Dean's demolished Porsche was on newspaper front pages all over the country, along with the tragic tale of what had happened.

Rolf Wütherich, a German mechanic who looked after Dean's cars, had been sitting in the passenger's seat. Bill "Big Bastard" Hickman, an actor and an action-film stuntman, loved fast cars, just as Jimmy did. That day he had been following them in Dean's Ford Country Squire station wagon. A black-and-white Ford Tudor turned left into his path; Jimmy didn't see it in time, and in the wreckage, he died in Hickman's arms. According to Hickman, the Ford had crossed the center line at the junction of Routes 466 and 41 near the town of Cholame.

In Jean's life, the silence that followed this news was violent and definitive. He was devastated. Once more, he had lost a friend, a brother who understood him. It was almost like losing a limb, and he was afraid of having to limp by on his own in a world where he had just barely learned to walk. Would he ever get over it?

Jimmy was too young to die, he repeated to himself in desperation.

His wife, Donna, embraced him; she had never seen him so shaken. *You have to believe in yourself,* she said to him. He told himself the same thing, but he felt like a stupid child, paralyzed by a fear that he had already known before, a feeling of powerlessness before a fate he could neither change nor understand.

He knew he had to continue, but the strength to pick up the pieces would have to come from inside him. If he let the tragedy carry him away, he would never have the energy to get back on track, to keep pushing ahead.

Growl you may, but go you must.
You have to keep going. You have to.

From his brother, he had learned to never give up. From his friend Jimmy, to always look forward, to shoot for the impossible. He couldn't let Jimmy Dean's sudden death put an end to his dreams for the restaurant. Jean Leon wouldn't be daunted. He owed that much to his friend. He would never abandon their dream.

CHAPTER 7

The death of Jimmy Dean, on September 30, 1955, didn't only leave Jean without his friend—a friend like none other—it also left him without a moneyman. A devastating yet familiar solitude fell over him. He knew he couldn't give up. But he had no funds of his own to open the restaurant. In moments like this, Jean would shut himself away, head in his hands, ruminating, and then not even Donna could reach him. But she had an idea, a name, and she knew it was just the thing to get Jean out of his mood.

"Karl," she said to him as he looked up from his morning paper. "Karl Kaetel."

Karl was the husband of her sister, Vera. He was a lawyer, and Jean often asked him for advice on legal and personal matters. Karl was close, he was family—someone Jean could trust. Moreover, he had money to spare. He just might be the perfect partner.

"You're a genius," he said to Donna, reaching across the table to grab her hand.

Karl didn't need too much information or time to let the idea marinate. He already knew his way around the business world. Jean asked him to be his partner and Karl accepted, putting up $3,500 to match the amount Jean had fronted. Donna contributed the last thousand so they could reach the $8,000 Joe Amor was asking for. Once that was done, they had a restaurant on their hands.

The next goal was clear. "We need to distinguish ourselves from the competition," Jean Leon told Emilio. Donna, who wanted to be a part of the restaurant's opening, agreed.

"It goes without saying," Donna observed, "that the quality of the food and service will be what makes or breaks us—but we can't forget the little details. And when I talk about the little details, I mean things like the furniture, the painting on the walls, the lighting, even the scent of the place, the music, the way the tables are laid out."

"But none of what you're saying matters if there's not a good menu. The food's got to be excellent," Emilio replied.

"Sure. The kitchen is essential. But normally, the guest doesn't enter the kitchen," Donna reminded him, smiling.

"I get what you're trying to say," Jean cut in. "The layout, the arrangement of the furniture, the people who are going to wait on you."

"Exactly," Donna said. "I'm talking about things you might not even notice, that make your first impression not just good, but great! That's what we've got to focus on. We want love at first sight—right, Jean?"

Donna winked at her husband, and Emilio laughed. It was nice to see them like that: two years into their relationship, going strong, with a passion in common. Often, when he stayed late in the kitchen, perfecting his recipes, or on the drive home in the early hours of the morning, Emilio's thoughts would turn to them, and he would imagine a future when the restaurant was up and running, and he would have time to be a devoted husband and father himself.

But for now, his every waking moment was devoted to La Scala—his uncle had chosen to name it after the greatest opera house in the world, and like musicians on the rehearsal stage, they had to get every detail down pat. For Emilio, that meant creating a top-notch menu, something that stood out, with exquisite, original, and unpredictable dishes, painstakingly prepared and plated, using only the very finest ingredients.

The opening was grueling. They couldn't just stick with their old purveyors: Jean had a vision, and Emilio did, too, and sometimes the products just weren't good enough for the restaurant they had in mind. That meant bad blood when he had to break relationships Emilio's uncle had spent decades cementing.

Then there was the staff. People came in with bad habits from their previous jobs, so Jean and Emilio had their task cut out for them: there could be no lazing around, no chitchat, no half measures. They knew the clientele they were aiming for, and those people wouldn't put up with mediocrity. Jean drilled the servers on the wine, how to stand, how to hold a serviette, while Emilio struggled to convince the cooks that his way was the right way, and that every single dish had to be timed, measured, and meticulously executed. All this amid the comings and goings of inspectors, builders, deliverymen, the press, and more than one curious onlooker.

The group worked scrupulously on two fronts: while Emilio continued to develop his ideas in the kitchen with Donna and Jean's blessing, the couple tried to give the place a special spirit. They worked hard, and there was a price to pay. La Scala took up so much energy and time that it clashed with their plans to start a family—and those plans were already well underway. Donna had gotten pregnant before construction had even begun. Now eight months along, she could no longer bear the strain, and while Jean spent more and more time at the restaurant, she found herself at home alone, hoping that soon she'd have back the husband she needed to be a father to their child.

On April 1, 1956, at 9455 Santa Monica Boulevard, in the heart of Beverly Hills, on the ground floor of the former offices of First National Bank, in a place once owned by Joe Amor, La Scala restaurant opened its doors. It wasn't too far from the beach—Jimmy would have liked that—and near luxurious Rodeo Drive. The design reflected nearly every idea the two friends had originally come up with: a prominent bar; private dining rooms for the stars; large, well-spaced tables, protected from the gazes of curious onlookers, with red leather upholstery on the chairs and booths. It had the feel of a private club, but with an almost-baroque exuberance conceived for comfort and elegance that would allow guests privacy while also leaving them free to mingle—to see and be seen.

Donna's attention to detail was reflected in the objects scattered around the dining room. From sculptures—like Houdon's bust of George Washington—to the vases and china straight from the factories in Limoges. There was hardwood wherever you looked. But the crown jewel of the space was the wine—exquisite bottles crammed into every corner. The list would expand constantly, eventually reaching thirty thousand bottles.

Jean looked around, glowing with satisfaction. He had done it. Jimmy would've been so proud, he was sure of it.

The first customer of the night entered: a tall, blond, elegant man, well built, with a clueless and incredulous air. Jean Leon recognized him immediately and rushed out to meet him.

"Arthur?"

"Jean? Jean Leon?"

Arthur Loew was the grandson of Marcus Loew, founder and proprietor of Metro-Goldwyn-Mayer.

"I didn't know you had opened a restaurant here, on Little Santa Monica. Congrats!"

Arthur Loew knew Jean Leon from his days at Villa Capri. They were the same age, they had gotten along right away, and both of them had been friends with Jimmy Dean.

"It's a hell of a good sign that you're our very first customer," Leon told him, waving toward the tables. "Pick the one you like best."

Loew headed for a round table in a corner close to the bar. Leon pulled out his chair for him and handed him the menu once he'd sat down.

"What do you recommend?"

"Don't bother ordering. Let me take care of it," Jean said.

Jean Leon still kept his Spanish origins secret from most people, but he had confided in Arthur one night when he was serving him. The MGM producer had a yen, almost a devotion, for anything that came from Spain—especially for the food, which he loved. Jean sent out the best—every dish he thought might make the man smile, with the finest wines to match. After Arthur had finished eating, Jean went over to check on him and make sure everything had been to his liking.

"Congratulations, Jean. Everything was fantastic. I'll do publicity for you, you can be sure of it!"

"Thanks, Arthur. I appreciate it. I won't lie to you, we need customers like you wouldn't believe."

"I'll be talking about La Scala to *tutti quanti.*"

With smiles and hugs, Jean Leon said goodbye to their first and only guest on opening night. That was the one time La Scala was ever empty.

The competition in Los Angeles was ferocious. But La Scala distinguished itself from the pack right away with its fine Mediterranean cooking, drawing on a wide variety of culinary traditions, prepared from the finest raw materials. Even those first months, when they were drowning in debt, they never lowered the quality of their ingredients. They didn't mind paying high prices if it meant their customers got the best.

And as they knew, the more the ingredients cost, the more exquisite the flavors. Their cheese list became world class. Jean had a weakness for the stuff, especially gorgonzola. Deliveries came in directly from Italy: once a month, they sent off to Lombardy for gorgonzola *dolce* and *piccante*, and their purveyor shipped them straight to the California coast. They served the cheeses as an appetizer along with house-baked bread, black olives, and endive leaves in olive oil, or as a dessert with seasonal fruits.

It didn't take long for word to get around. Soon enough, the restaurant was a reference point, a place where many faces known and loved found their little oasis of company and privacy.

Before the first month was out, Gary Cooper, Tyrone Power, David Niven, Gregory Peck, Lauren Bacall, Clark Gable, Rock Hudson, and Warren Beatty had come in, the last of these with his sister, Shirley MacLaine. A big boost to the restaurant was Jack Paar's recommendation live on the *Tonight Show*, NBC's most-watched program. He said he had dined there, that the food was majestic, and that it was the new favorite haunt of every star in Hollywood. That was the kind of advertising you couldn't dream of, and you certainly couldn't pay for.

Jean Leon wasn't the only one who was coming up in the world. The little group of actors who used to hang out at his old job were no longer promising youngsters; many had become Hollywood's biggest stars. Now that James Dean was gone, Leon had started opening up more and making friends with other members of the group. They missed Jimmy just as he did.

Nat was one of them—Natalie Wood, the girl from the group whom everyone, more or less, was in love with. Sadly, it was always unrequited, because for years she'd only had eyes for RJ—Robert John Wagner. Jean and Nat grew so close, they were soon like brother and sister. Jean even started a new tradition at La Scala: he added the actress's favorite dish to the menu, a pasta she had fallen in love with. In Italy they called it *penne lisce*, but immigrants to the New World had dubbed those hollow noodles, cut at an angle on both ends, *mostaccioli*, which meant "little mustaches." Emilio would bake them with his signature meat sauce, until a fine crust formed on the mozzarella over the top of it. The actress was mad for it, it was all she ever wanted, and they wound up naming it after her: mostaccioli Natalie.

The second dish Jean put on the menu in honor of a customer was dedicated to a promising, rather solitary young man who reminded him so much of James Dean that he couldn't help but take a liking to him—an up-and-coming actor named Paul Newman. When Newman visited La Scala, he always ordered a celery salad with salt and pepper for dinner, along with a cold beer to wash it down.

Jean often stopped by to chat with him during these meals. Paul was struggling with a decision just then.

"I can't accept it, Jean," Newman repeated over and over. "It isn't my role."

"But you have to," Jean said in a firm tone. "You couldn't think of a better way to pay homage to Jimmy."

"I feel like I'm stepping into someone else's territory."

"Don't be a fool! Jimmy's gone, and he's not coming back. Who's going to play that role better than you?"

That role in question was Rocky Graziano in *Somebody up There Likes Me*. It had been meant for Dean, but after his tragic accident, they offered it to Newman. Ironically, James Dean's death helped make Paul Newman a star. But if it had to happen, why not to him? He had known Dean well, they had both come from the TV world, they were friends, and they shared a strong mutual respect.

"I remember the screen tests we did for *East of Eden*," Newman said with a lost look in his eyes, reproducing the dialogue that Kazan had told them to have ready. Jean worried that the pride Newman should be feeling over his newfound success would be tinged forever with guilt and regret.

Newman's blue eyes turned mournful as he looked at Jean sitting next to him. Trying to cheer him up, Jean quickly changed the subject.

"Say what you will, but this isn't going to cut it!" Jean said with a chuckle, pointing at what was left of his friend's salad. Newman looked at him. "You can make the film or not, but what you're not going to do is keep coming in here and eating like a rabbit," Jean went on. "From now on, you come to my restaurant, I choose your meal. Whether you want to be a star or not is your call. But you'll damn sure eat like one here."

And that was how, not long afterward, the famous grenadine of beef à la Paul Newman showed up on La Scala's menu. Two juicy beef medallions, grilled rare, with house-made hollandaise, broccoli, and whipped potatoes. The secret was the Spanish paprika Emilio imported for the sauce—that, and lots of butter for the potatoes.

Sure enough, Newman took that fateful role, and his memorable performance won him the respect and recognition of critics and the public. Thanks to Leon, his palate won over more than a few gastronomes as well. In the process, Leon taught Newman a lesson: his tastes could change, and so could those of the audience.

"Jimmy Dean was unforgettable. You and I will always remember him, and the spectators will, too. But you've got talent, Paul. And if you put it out there, audiences will know how to appreciate it. You deserve to be recognized."

It was clear to quite a few discerning critics and customers that La Scala deserved to be recognized, too—the quality of its cooking certainly warranted it. Never far from the grill, Emilio Nuñez was sharpening his talents and making a name for himself, and he was now the youngest executive chef in Los Angeles. He had natural drive, and he had the talent, but more than that, he had the desperation well known to every Spaniard living in exile during the Franco years. Occasionally Emilio would receive letters from home detailing the repression, the poverty, the misery; even speaking Galician, the language of his province, could get a person a beating at the hands of the fascist police. Now and again, someone would straggle in looking for a job, speaking broken English, and Emilio would take them on as a dishwasher or prep cook just to hear the news from back home. It was never good, and Emilio realized he'd been given a golden opportunity. He had escaped that life, and now he had a chance to build himself a new one.

The dishes Emilio prepared under Leon's supervision certainly caught the attention of their customers. The pasta was made in-house: "Pasta Fatta in Casa," the sign said at the entrance, and everybody was wild about his ravioli, fettuccine, lasagna, and cannelloni. He had learned the technique from his uncle, whose Italian *mamma* had helped him get his start in the restaurant business. But Emilio had gone a step further, traveling to Italy when he could and having the best ingredients shipped to him: tomatoes from San Marzano, oil from Liguria. When he couldn't find buffalo mozzarella in LA, he arranged to have Scandinavian Airlines fly it over.

Still, Emilio never forgot Galicia; the memory of it was in his blood, and that differentiated La Scala from the French-influenced repertory of other restaurants in the area. He knew better than to drown a good piece of fish in sauce; he knew how to judge seafood by the feel and smell; and he knew not to fill his fryers with the cheap industrial oils and shortenings that had begun to invade restaurant kitchens.

La Scala was unique—Jean and Emilio were unique—and that caught the press's eye. The influential food critic for *Cosmopolitan* ate there and then arranged a meeting with Jean Leon the same week to ask some questions before he wrote his review.

Leon was on edge when the critic showed up on the assigned day with a photographer.

"We need a signature dish from the menu," the critic said with the indifference of someone used to giving orders. "Maybe antipasti, something that represents the essence of what you do."

It was *Cosmo*. No one dared to contradict them. Jean Leon went along with their requests until they proposed having a stranger they had brought along with them pose as the chef in photographs instead of Emilio.

"What are you talking about?" shouted Leon. The imposter was, to be fair, the perfect image of a chef: a mature man of sturdy build, with a substantial mustache whose curled tips pointed at the ceiling, and the standard *toque blanche* on his head.

Emilio, on the other hand, was short and squat, not much more than a kid. He had thick hair and sideburns, and an eternal five-o'clock shadow. He didn't care much for the limelight, so he found the magazine's scheme hilarious. But Leon was livid.

"That shows a lack of respect for my chef and a lack of respect for your readers!" Leon objected, refusing to let the reporter explain himself. For him, there was nothing to be discussed.

"But Mr. Leon, neither the customers nor our readers know your chef." The critic couldn't understand why Leon had a problem with the idea. "And I'm sorry, but Mr. Nuñez's image isn't what comes into people's heads when they think *chef*."

"You're goddamn right he isn't. Emilio Nuñez is a king, and that's the entire point: neither he nor our cooking resemble anyone or anything else."

Jean threw the *ingrates* out of his restaurant. That was the word he used, and it was the softest one he could come up with.

"Emilio, this won't stand, I promise you that! The press is going to give us the attention we deserve, and they're going to do it on our terms."

"Forget it, Jean. It's not a big deal."

"I swear to you! Or else my name's not Jean Leon!"

"Don't be silly. You and I both know your name's not Jean," Emilio said with a smile. "Come on, let it go. When you cool down, you'll see it differently, believe me."

Emilio disappeared behind the swinging door to the kitchen. But Leon wouldn't give up that easily. No one could beat the Lion for obstinacy and determination.

He had to control everything, down to the final details. That was Jean's conclusion after the dustup with *Cosmopolitan*. La Scala was his kingdom, and he was the one who called the shots. Nothing missed his attention, and he oversaw everything with an iron resolve that soon became obsessive.

For the next few days, late into the night, he kept trying to think of some original way to get press; he barely slept for a week. But his tenacity led him to a solution. It was imaginative, and it exceeded all expectation.

"We're going to be in the *Los Angeles Times*!" he blurted out one day in the kitchen.

"How so?" Emilio said, his attention focused on the last row of tickets still hanging in the window. It was the hardest part of the day—not the rush, when everyone knew they were busy and had to work like mad, but just after, when the cooks were taking turns going out back for a coffee and a smoke but the pressure was still on to get the last round out in a timely manner.

"From now on, they're going to call us the Ritz and Escoffier of Beverly Hills. I came up with that on the phone with the head of the food section, and he liked the comparison. When he heard it, he decided to do an article on the restaurant and how we run the business."

"So we're supposed to be some kind of Laurel and Hardy now? You're the skinny guy and I'm the fat one? Give me a break." Emilio frowned.

"No, man, no! You fool!"

Leon's fascination with history and art had made him think of the idea, just as long before it had suggested to him a new name. Again, he was aiming for the stars, to reach the lofty heights where César Ritz and Auguste Escoffier, the fathers of modern restaurant service, had stood. Those two pioneers had worked together at the Grand Hotel National in Lucerne, in Switzerland, César Ritz as the maître d' and Auguste Escoffier as the chef.

"They were just like us, but at the beginning of the century," Leon explained to his suspicious partner. "They created a new restaurant concept."

Like us. Leon ran down the list. Service: exquisite. Kitchen: groundbreaking. Wines: magnificent. Food: unforgettable. The result for Ritz and Escoffier was a refined, exclusive restaurant with a smaller number of tables for a very select clientele.

"Together, they founded the Savoy hotel in London, the Grand Hotel in Rome, and Ritzes all over the world, in Paris, Cairo, Johannesburg, Madrid . . . They were visionaries."

Like me, Jean thought. Since Jimmy's death, he hadn't found anyone to share his dreams with, and he didn't like meeting resistance from the people he was close to. He bristled at the look on Emilio's face just then. Donna was no better; she too seemed to think there was something pretentious in all that ambition.

This Ritz-Escoffier tandem he wanted to form with Emilio Nuñez wasn't only meant to take La Scala to the top, but even to expand from the restaurant business into broader and more diverse fields. He refused to be content with what he had. And he was willing to do anything to get what he wanted.

"Emilio, this connection you and I have is the same as with those two geniuses," Leon said, nodding to convince himself there was truth in his words, in the hopes he could soon convince others. "And here in Hollywood, where image is everything, it'll help us, comparing ourselves to two guys who had success and fame all over the world. Everyone knows their names."

Emilio threw up his hands in resignation, and Leon took that as a victory.

"They cooked for all the celebrities of the day: the Prince of Wales, Count Nigra, Sarah Bernhardt, the leading ladies of the stage and the demimonde . . ."

"I never cooked for any king!" Emilio protested.

"I know, Emilio," Leon conceded with a sigh. "But you're like Escoffier, you have the kind of instinct only the great masters have. You can't see it, because it comes from inside you, but believe me, what you do, it touches the body as well as the spirit. And you do it with simplicity, and you know how to adapt your cooking to new flavors."

Emilio shrugged.

"Caesar, the die is cast. Monsieur Escoffier at your service!"

Emilio bowed theatrically, and the two men broke into laughter. This was his way of blessing Jean's PR strategy. Once more, Jean had gotten what he wanted: he was convincing, and he wouldn't let anyone stand in his way. You had to follow along with him, but he did know how to listen—and how to be quiet when the occasion demanded. That was part of his charm, and the charm of La Scala itself.

Leon never spread rumors or fed the gossip mill about gatherings that took place at La Scala. He kept his integrity, and that brought him closer and closer to his famous friends—the stars, the cinema magnates, the occasional politician. With his carefully managed image and his affable, boyish face, his stark features and animated eyes, he practiced to a T what he had learned at Villa Capri: discretion, trust, likability. Mike Romanoff, the charismatic owner of Romanoff's restaurant, had told him once, "Half of a restaurant's atmosphere depends on its owner."

And what was attractive about La Scala was Jean Leon—his presence, his ability to please, his power—and he was always there.

He played the part of the ideal host to the hilt, with attention and deference, never flaunting the restaurant's luxury or exclusivity. He knew all the regulars by name and tried to be sure there was always a table ready for them. And if there wasn't, he would make one—literally.

One night, when La Scala was packed to bursting as usual, a familiar face came in.

"Warren!"

When Jean saw the actor, he went straight up to greet him. Warren Beatty had been a loyal guest ever since his future costar from *Splendor in the Grass*, Natalie Wood, had introduced him to Jean.

"You got a table?" the actor asked, looking around dubiously at the buzzing restaurant.

He was right to be skeptical. It was clear to both that not another soul could squeeze in that night.

"For you, Warren, always," Leon said reassuringly.

"Where would that be . . . in the kitchen?"

Jean Leon's face lit up. He asked Beatty to wait at the bar while he vanished into the back of the restaurant, calling over his shoulder, "Have a drink. On the house."

The actor elbowed his way in among the guests seated at the hefty barstools and leaned his elbow against the leather-padded rail, pulling over an ashtray and eyeing the bottles lined up on shelves beneath rows of freshly polished glasses.

A few minutes later, Jean beckoned him back toward the swinging kitchen doors.

"Where are you taking me, Jean?" Beatty asked.

"It's a surprise," Jean said, amused.

The actor was perplexed, and his face showed it. Then Jean opened the doors to the kitchen.

"Voilà!" Leon exclaimed, beaming with satisfaction. "We've got a new table, and it's just for you."

In one corner, between dry storage and the door, the table where the staff usually sat for their breaks had been festooned with a white cloth, a vase with four flowers, and a little lamp. There were two complete settings there, with plates, chargers, and glasses for water and wine. The employees couldn't believe their eyes, nor could Beatty.

"You're one of a kind, Jean. Who else could have come up with this!" Beatty said, giving him a few friendly slaps on the back.

"The credit is yours, Warren, you're the one who said it. I had to do something, there was no way I could just throw you out on the street," Leon replied.

"This is a real privilege, eating back here, where the magic happens!" Beatty said.

From then on, that improvised table, fruit of a moment's necessity, became the most sought-after one in the restaurant. And the most exclusive.

Again, Emilio had to grin and bear yet another of Jean's quirks. He peered over from behind the grill, shaking his head at this gamble, but luckily for them both, Jean always seemed to hit the mark. But then, Emilio had his part in that, too. He always knew how to manage these whims so that they ended with more happiness than grief.

Soon enough, the two men were celebrating the restaurant's fourth anniversary. The duo functioned like a well-oiled machine as long as the chef held on to his place as the conscience of Jean, who was getting harder and harder to handle.

"Luckily, I don't ever pay you any mind," Jean told Emilio. "And see, here we are celebrating it."

Jean never left the restaurant—or at least it seemed that way to Emilio, who was always eager to rush home at the end of the night. For him, the restaurant was an investment, a place to work and hone his craft, but he got no thrill out of seeing or being seen. When the day was done, he treasured his relaxation at home. Jean, on the other hand, liked to linger, to break down how the evening's service had gone, to plan ahead for events to come, to dream for the future.

Often Emilio had the unpleasant feeling that Jean wasn't so much lingering at a place he loved as avoiding being somewhere else: his home. Emilio missed Jean's wife, Donna, even if Jean didn't seem to.

But the chef didn't voice his worries to Jean. Instead he focused on those small battles that he had at least a chance of winning. Like Jean's gruff manner with his employees, the very opposite of the kindness he offered his customers. While Jean treated his guests with kid gloves, he managed his staff with an iron fist, and that often caused problems. He felt he could demand the maximum from them because *he* gave *his* all and he offered the best clientele and the biggest tips in all of Hollywood.

"It's a matter of principle," he said. And that was that. His friends, from Emilio to big stars like James Dean, had reproached his obsessiveness and his demanding nature—but as the restaurant grew, he started to cultivate those qualities intentionally. He perfected the Humphrey Bogart stare, which froze the blood of anyone who tried to contradict him.

La Scala was the world for Jean Leon, and he gave it all the time and energy it required, at the expense of everything else. Everything else being, principally, Donna and their two children.

He had become one of the *beautiful people*, and that was what mattered most to him. At seven every morning, he was already headed to the restaurant. He would have his coffee at one of the booths while he waited for the first deliveries. In theory, he left the closing duties to a manager or headwaiter, but in practice, some VIP always kept him long after the doors were locked. He would come home past midnight, liquor on his breath, bragging of how he'd shared a cognac with this or that celebrity, and he never noticed Donna's bitterness, nor how it faded gradually into resignation.

With time, his family became a thing to be referred to, but not to be taken care of, and he worried more about thumb smudges on the silver and how the servers carried the plates than whether the strain of his absence was pushing his wife over the edge. Jean was consumed by what he felt was his true calling: feeding the stars' bodies and souls. And he was a master host: he was happy to let them take center stage while he observed from the wings, making sure to keep gawkers and the press on the sidelines. On the rare occasions when stories did leak out, Jean was never accused of using the stars' names and stories to buy press for his restaurant. More often than not, the leakers were the stars themselves, so everyone was satisfied. And Jean remained atop his small kingdom, the silent, benevolent monarch.

The restaurant became the place everyone wanted to go, just to see who was there. It was a barometer for celebrities' success. And all the credit went to the men running the kitchen and the dining room: Emilio Nuñez at the stove, Jean Leon on the floor. A team that shined as brightly as the stars who showed up night after night at La Scala.

CHAPTER 8

"Donna?"

"Yes, she's on the other line," the headwaiter repeated.

"Don't you see I can't talk right now! Tell her—"

"I'm sorry, Jean, but she said it's urgent."

The warmth of that July morning wasn't what had provoked Jean Leon's heated reaction as he stood in the middle of the large dining room reserved for the Democratic delegation, who would be dining there that night. The team of waiters following his orders for the preparations stopped at once. Everyone knew Jean couldn't stand interruptions, and it wasn't the first time they'd seen their boss fly off the handle.

"Goddamn it!" He cursed, rolling his eyes. "I'll take it in my office."

He left in a fury, slamming the door so hard the bottles and wineglasses decorating the dining room clinked loudly in protest.

"What is it, Donna?" he asked impatiently.

"I'm going to the hospital."

"What? Are you all right? What happened?" His fury abated slightly as he bombarded his wife with questions.

"It's Jean-Georges. He fell on the playground at school and broke his arm. They took him to Saint John's."

"But . . . it's only his arm, right?"

"Yes." Even in that single word, Donna couldn't conceal the disappointment in her voice, which quickly became more strident. "Yes, Jean. *Only* his arm. I called you because you need to go home and take care of Cécile. She's too little to come to the hospital with us."

"What? Are you crazy? We have an extremely important group of customers to take care of in a few hours, Donna. You know that."

"Then I'll bring her to the restaurant and someone there can take care of her," his wife said cuttingly.

"Impossible, Donna. It's not like we have extra staff just sitting around—everyone's already working like crazy. A two-year-old kid can't be here . . . Why don't you take her to your sister's?"

"Of course. You're right. I'll just dump her off on Vera again. Thanks so much, Jean!"

Donna hung up.

Leon counted to five and let out a breath. *It's like she thinks I'm doing this on purpose.* Maybe if she had called him on a less busy day . . . It was true that Donna took care of raising the two kids almost on her own, and he knew she resented the time he spent away from his family—all day in the restaurant, countless late nights, forever at the whim of the needs of the stars. His family always came second to La Scala, and they all knew it. That persistent headache of his grew worse.

He concentrated on a point behind his eye sockets, breathed deeply, counted to five again, and let the matter drop. He went back to ordering his team around the banquet room, trying to keep his anxiety about the evening's event under wraps so it wouldn't affect the staff.

He'd had his fair share of important guests before, VIPs of all sorts. But tonight was different. Tonight, the person likely to become the next president of the United States, John F. Kennedy, would be there. That same month—the very next night, in fact—JFK, the young senator from Massachusetts, would be named the Democratic nominee at the party's convention right there in the city. He would be facing the Republican Richard Nixon in the election, and Nixon would have the advantage of his eight years as vice president under Eisenhower. Experience, homespun rhetoric, and mediocrity would be up against a six-foot-tall senator with good looks, elegant clothes, and a magnetic smile full of ivory teeth that gleamed out from a face and body carefully tanned at the family home in Palm Beach.

"They've talked this place up so much that I couldn't wait to try it myself," JFK said to Jean when they arrived that night.

Jean Leon, who was more than used to dealing with the most charming personalities of the Hollywood establishment, felt unusually small in front of that man, even with his kind and familiar manner. Jean knew right away why he'd been called upon to lead the country. Never, since his arrival in America, had Jean taken an interest in politics, but for some reason the upcoming elections seemed like his elections, too. He felt a kinship with the candidate that he couldn't ignore.

Kennedy was more like an expression of Hollywood vitality than of Washington, with its distant formality. The daily papers were filled with unsettling reports of the world dividing into blocs, of the arms race, of a climate of fear threatening a nation tired from more than a decade of armed conflict—a nation that now, in the 1960s, was looking to leave all that behind. Kennedy represented youth, determination, and the recuperation of the American way of life. And the electorate was ready to embrace that. *I wouldn't bet against him,* Jean thought.

That night at La Scala, the future president and two of the Kennedy brothers, Robert and Edward, would go over the details of the nomination. Tagging along were several movers and shakers from the party, like Lyndon B. Johnson and Adlai Stevenson, as well as Hollywood figures who supported the candidacy.

Confirmed attendees included Liz Taylor, Marlon Brando, Robert Wagner, Natalie Wood, Peter Lawford, and his wife, Pat Kennedy, the candidate's sister. All of them were friends and regulars of Jean Leon's. The Lawford-Kennedys had been coming in ever since La Scala first opened its doors. They were the ones who had insisted on holding

Kennedy's nomination party there—but to avoid word getting out, they had only told the candidate the day before. Leon was a master at dealing with contingencies, especially avoiding leaks to the press. No journalists, no feature stories, no unwanted photos. A celebration like that would set the press on fire, but nothing would ever come out except the menu and a few images Leon and Lawford had authorized.

"Kennedy had a salad, fettuccine Leon, and a steak. He didn't order dessert. He had a coffee to finish," the owner of La Scala told a group of journalists waiting outside when the night was over.

"Did the senator enjoy his dinner?" one reporter asked.

"Of course!" Leon assured her. "He asked me to make the same thing tomorrow!"

Leon's brief appearance ended with chuckles. Everyone seemed satisfied: the press because they could fill out their articles with the few details he'd given them, and John Fitzgerald Kennedy because he'd found a place where he could be himself, a place he would return to on future trips to the West Coast. Not as a mere politician, but as president of the United States.

Jean returned home elated. Long gone were the days of struggling to turn tables, of countless hours behind the wheel of a cab, of groveling for tips. He was rubbing shoulders with people who held the world in their hands. And he'd made it all by himself, he thought as he pulled into the drive. The lights were off and the house was quiet and dark. On the kitchen table lay a note telling him dinner was in the oven. But he wasn't hungry—he was eager to share the news of the big event with his wife. He poured two drinks, walked to the bedroom, flicked on the lights, and said, "I'm home!" Donna looked up at him with swollen eyelids. "Turn off the light."

"But Donna, you've got to listen to me, we didn't miss a beat, and everybody was there, I mean everybody . . ."

"Jean, cut off the light," Donna said.

"This guy's going to be president, Donna. You're not listening to me—"

"No, Jean, you're not listening to me. I'm tired."

"Fine," he said and returned to the living room alone, shutting the door quietly behind him.

CHAPTER 9

"This table was Warren Beatty's idea," Leon explained to Sinatra, who had just wandered into his kitchen. "Now everyone wants to eat here, in the kitchen."

That night, six years since Leon's departure from Villa Capri, Sinatra had finally decided to dine at La Scala. He showed up with his usual retinue, on this occasion four men and two women, all of whom stood discreetly at one end of the bar. The bartender took care of them while a waiter accompanied the singer into the kitchen, where Leon was going over the list of reservations for the next day. The way he moved through the place, Sinatra seemed like a regular, but in fact it was the first time he'd set foot in the place. Sinatra and Leon greeted each other by name and shook hands, a bit too formally, dispassionately.

The maître d' came over and nodded as Leon gave the orders, moving his arms with determination, like an orchestra director. Draped in an immaculate suit, with a dark jacket and matching tie, Leon was a far cry from the bumbling, obliging young waiter Sinatra had gotten a job for so long ago, the one who used to struggle to get a word out in English. But he still had that innocent baby face that belied his years, that same clear-eyed stare, the natural elegance and kindness that had caught Frank's eye the day they met.

The kitchen table was set for two, with glasses for a wine Jean Leon opened himself, nodding approvingly after examining the cork. He served his guest first, then passed him the bottle to examine, as he'd seen Sinatra do so many times before—the original consummate host.

"A Barbaresco," Leon said. "A recommendation from someone who knows his way around wine. A case came in this morning. I'm thinking of putting it on the list."

Leon noticed his guest was acting shifty, but Frank was like that when he wasn't in control. Leon knew from experience that direct questions wouldn't get him anywhere. It was better to let the conversation flow toward his old friend's interests, without forcing him to say anything.

Anyway, Sinatra was content to let himself be flattered, and that had always been one of Leon's talents. After a few minutes, the two settled into an easy back-and-forth. Leon told him—as though continuing a chat from the day before—how they made the fresh pasta. The wine was going down well. He recommended Frank try the fettuccine—Emilio made it just the way he liked, the former waiter told him.

Little by little, the Voice relaxed. Maybe it was the food—the kitchen table in La Scala boasted a culinary repertoire that could disarm the gruffest character. Or perhaps it was the wine that loosened him up, especially after the arrival of the second bottle (and not the last)—a fantastic Bardolino, a beautiful ruby-colored pour with notes of balsamic and cherry.

"You and Donna still together?"

Sinatra had a knack for that: remembering the names of all the people he cared about, along with their spouses, exes, and children. In case anyone doubted it, he wanted to make clear that he knew everything about everyone, that nothing got past him. Then again, that subject—family relations—touched both men's weak spots. For the first time, Jean didn't know how to react. He didn't even try to look convincing when he nodded. The singer gazed at Leon sympathetically. He dropped his forced indifference, leaned over to refill the two glasses, and offered a toast:

"To our wives, who haven't driven us completely nuts." Sinatra's tone was impish. "Unlike Marilyn with poor DiMaggio, remember?"

"Of course I do," Leon said, toasting as well, laughing as he thought back to that night. "I heard that a rumor made the rounds in the editors' room of *Confidential* that Marilyn actually *was* at those apartments that night."

"Hal Schaefer himself told me the same thing sometime later. They were both there, and they heard the whole thing. He said to me, 'If you guys had caught us, I'd be a dead man right now,'" Sinatra recalled.

"I saw you guys when you left and when you got back. I'd say the poor bastard was right," Leon added.

Sinatra lit another cigarette while the previous one went on smoldering in the ashtray.

"I've always valued loyalty and discretion," Sinatra said, taking the conversation down a different path. "That night, you showed me you were someone I could trust."

"I guess I've learned it's important to be able to keep a secret," Leon said. "Years back, someone saved my life, and he told me knowing how to keep a secret is what makes a person strong."

"You got that right, Jean." Sinatra paused and finished his cigarette with two last drags. "I gotta say, you've done pretty well for yourself," he conceded, taking a quick look around the restaurant. "Who would have thought it . . ."

"I learned from the best," Jean said.

When he said *the best*, he meant Sinatra—but also one of his sidekicks, Jimmy Van Heusen. After Jean's role in the high jinks with DiMaggio and the police, his star had risen, and more and more people started offering him work. On nights when Villa Capri was closed, Sinatra sometimes hired Jean as a driver and waiter for private parties at the home of Jimmy Van Heusen, where Sinatra was staying after divorcing Ava Gardner.

Van Heusen—Chet or Chester to his friends—was Sinatra's composer and songwriter. He had a gruff appearance that didn't match his personality. Tall and stocky, with a thick neck, shaved head, and deep voice, he looked more like a roughneck than the puppy dog that he was. He was an elegant dresser with a gift for gab. He was strangely magnetic—especially with the ladies, who thought him a gentleman, and he could play them as easily as he played the piano.

Sinatra threw many a private party in Chet's home, and there, Jean got a rare peek into the less glamorous side of the Hollywood myth. He saw stars and political bigwigs lose their grace and their sense of shame. Jean was discreet, he forgot what he had seen and never repeated what he was told—not even to Donna. That reserve put up yet another wall between him and his wife. What ground he gained among the celebrities, seducing them with his unobtrusive manner, he lost with Donna.

At Van Heusen's house, everybody loved to gather out on the patio. At the bar in front of the pool, Chet would down his usual glass of bourbon and give advice to the very young and receptive Jean Leon, who soaked in every word.

"Don't ever make a show of yourself like the rest of these clowns." Chet jutted his chin out toward the multitude gathered around the pool, not calling out anyone in particular.

The kid could have written a rule book for making it in Hollywood with all the guidance Van Heusen gave him: *Keep an eye on your conduct, at work and outside of it. Know your business like the back of your hand, so no one can tell you you're wrong. If you get in a fight, ask for forgiveness, even if you're in the right—your friendships matter more than your pride. Don't drink too much . . .* (He would say this when his glass, the only one he allowed himself, was empty except for the ice cubes, which he liked to savor. He'd keep them in his mouth, and before they melted, he'd crush them in a couple of bites and swallow them down.) *Leave the party early. Don't hog the spotlight, but don't go unnoticed, either. Don't try to persuade people with words; let your actions speak for you. Don't do anything just for the sake of recognition. Be generous, and don't expect anything from it. Never break a promise. Dress nice, regardless of the occasion. Don't lower the bar for anyone. Don't judge and don't compromise. You can always do better. Chivalry never goes out of style.*

"Ah, and then there's the golden rule: *ladies first.* You can measure a man's charisma by the smile of the woman on his arm."

When his glass was empty, Chet would go off to mingle with the group of well-known faces socializing around the pool. He knew everyone, and everyone greeted him. He knew their names, what they were after, what they liked, and what they dreamed of. He played to the hilt the role of host to the stars, friend to the stars, confidant of the stars. He had a way of bringing people together and of keeping out anyone who didn't fit in. He knew what he had to do and how he had to do it.

And Jean kept his eye on the ball. Those parties were where he learned how to adapt to his new culture, his new language, and his new world. A changing environment, a paradise filled with light, with goodwill, but also with risks. He learned to treat each person differently. He had an almost innate ability to do so, and in that world, it became an essential ingredient for his future triumphs. He called it the Chester Style: little by little, Jean took over the other man's mannerisms, behavior, turns of phrase—always putting his own personal stamp on them.

He had learned from the best, no doubt about it. Life lessons that would mark him forever. The first thing he grasped was if you want to be someone, you have to trust yourself.

Then, he learned that excellence means playing the roles you want to play in the places you want to be. Jean Leon began to mold himself to his ideal: the perfect host for the restaurant he aspired to run, and the American father of the family, the cocksure provider, the furthest thing possible from the naive immigrant he had been. He would adapt, with panache and sophistication, to the American way of life, and he would wind up making it his own.

And finally, he realized that if he wanted respect—if he really aspired to be respected like Sinatra—he would only get it by getting out from under Sinatra's thumb. That was what drove him to open La Scala six years ago. In Sinatra's eyes, that had been a betrayal. For years, Jean had known he needed to patch things up between them. And he would have to be the one to take the first step.

Ten days before the Voice showed up at La Scala, Jean had given him a call.

He had a problem, and he needed help. It was true that Frank was a stern guy who never forgot anything, but he was also a man of his word. Jean was sure he could still depend on him, despite the distance the past few years had put between them.

Jean Leon had just a few very faithful friends, and no enemies—or so he thought. La Scala's success had made some people envious and had led to more than one sticky situation, but he was proud to say he'd always gotten through them unharmed. Until that late night, ten days earlier, when he was shutting down the restaurant, lost in thought, as usual, and a noise outside caught his attention.

Ever since he'd put down roots in LA and wriggled out of his troubles with the army, both the Spanish one and the American one, he no longer worried about his past catching up with him. So when he locked the front door and two men grabbed him and shoved him into a dark, empty alley, his only reaction was utter confusion. One of them got behind him and wrapped his enormous arms around Jean's neck, squeezing him until he choked. The other started to smack him around, then dealt several hard blows to his belly, chest, and face. They let Jean's battered body fall to the ground just before he lost consciousness, and he stayed there on all fours.

"You've got the wrong guy," Leon shouted at them through split, bleeding lips.

One of them grabbed his right hand, and the other started breaking his fingers one by one. Leon howled in pain, tears misting his eyes. He had no idea why they were torturing him.

"What do you want from me?"

"This is from Mr. Durán," one of the thugs said after breaking the last of his fingers. "We'll be here tomorrow to collect on his debt. Ten thousand dollars."

The attackers picked him up and threw him against the wall one last time, then walked away slowly. *Durán? Durán?* Leon was shaken. As he struggled to get his bearings, an image flashed into his mind: a tubby, bald man with a mustache, wearing garish clothes. José Durán. Now he remembered. That flamboyant agent who had sent him off to Spain to entice the famous dancers Antonio and Rosario to come work in Hollywood. That was years ago—he had never spoken to Durán again, and after he started at Villa Capri, he had forgotten the whole affair. He had other things on his mind once he returned from Spain. But it wasn't that big a deal, was it? Surely not enough to send two thugs to beat him to a pulp.

After the men disappeared, Leon stumbled out onto the main street and caught a cab to the hospital. There they treated his injuries and put his broken hand in a splint. He would look for a solution to his new problem tomorrow. In the morning, he showed up at the restaurant battered and bruised, dragging one leg, and with sunglasses on to hide his two black eyes. He was dressed casually, in a shirt and jeans, not in his usual elegant suit. He was nearly unrecognizable, out of sorts, and obviously not in any shape to work. And yet there he was, at La Scala. As usual. He brushed off the maître d's anxious questions and gave him a careful set of instructions.

"If a couple of roughnecks come in here asking for me, you treat them like VIPs and come tell me, OK?"

Jean stumbled to his office, his little private island, where he went to gather his thoughts and plan new projects. He needed to ask for a favor. He collapsed into the armchair in an unlit corner. He remembered Frank's exact words to him: *If you ever need to solve a problem . . .* Well, Jean Leon had one, a big one. There are men who keep their word no matter how much time has passed. Frank was one of them. Leon picked up the phone and dialed.

Later that afternoon, Durán's men showed up at the restaurant, and were surprised at the courtesy and attention they received. Leon was buying time.

"Please, order whatever you like," the headwaiter said.

They ordered two whiskeys, but soon were being treated to champagne, oysters, Bordeaux—all of it on the house. The two goons softened up and failed to notice two other guys, even surlier than they were, leaning on the other end of the bar and watching their every move.

They introduced themselves to the bartender with the agreed-upon words: "We're Jean Leon's nephews."

After drinking more than their fill, Durán's men got out of hand, and the bartender asked them to leave. That was when Leon's "nephews" stepped in, offering to accompany them out. The thugs' manner changed when they saw the business end of a revolver pointed at them. The "nephews" took them out to a secluded back alley, administered a skillful pistol-whipping, and squeezed Durán's address out of them.

Located in the heights of Beverly Hills, José Durán's mansion was a true reflection of his personality: exaggerated, overblown, egotistical. It was a hulking domicile utterly lacking in any good taste or architectural discretion, a bizarre mix of styles for which *eclectic* could only be a euphemism. The "nephews" had no trouble identifying it from afar: dozens of spotlights made sure no one could miss it. They easily slipped past the scant security measures and found their target oblivious in his pool, floating on his back, eyes closed, like a corpse—as if anticipating what he had coming.

115

The two toughs couldn't have hoped for a better situation. Durán didn't even see the hand that pushed him underwater. It was powerful, and he couldn't get away. He splashed and flailed desperately, scratching at the hand and forearm that kept pushing him inexorably downward. He kicked violently, trying to swim away. He was running out of air. He was dying.

When Durán's legs stopped thrashing, the hand moved away, and the agent managed to raise his head above the water. He could barely breathe, and his eyes were blurry. Then he felt the two men grab him from behind, pick him up, and throw him onto the tiles beside the pool. A gruff voice threatened him.

"We're Jean Leon's nephews," was the first and last thing he heard.

Without further ado, the men left.

That same night, the police picked up two frightened men with bound hands close to the restaurant. An anonymous tip accused them of trying to extort a well-known restaurateur. Mission accomplished.

And now, Frank Sinatra and Jean Leon were together again, sharing the special table in the kitchen at La Scala, drinking into the wee hours of the morning, reminiscing and exchanging secrets the way they used to do on nights like that, making up for lost time.

"I guess you fixed that thing, right?" Sinatra asked him, pointing, with a very Sicilian gesture—Sicilian like Frank himself—at the bruise on Leon's cheek.

"Thanks to, uh . . . my *nephews* you sent over, yeah, that guy won't come bothering me again. I owe you one."

Their loyalty had been tested. And their friendship had passed with flying colors. Things were never quite the same, but after that long night they'd spent in the kitchen, sharing a bottle of wine and some old memories, Jean and his mentor were finally back on the same team.

CHAPTER 10

"Lawford called," Emilio told Jean one day when he arrived at the restaurant.

"Tonight?"

It was the summer of 1962. Emilio nodded, plainly worried about the huge order that had just been phoned in. For weeks, there had been rumors that the president was staying in Palm Springs, but Jean hadn't given the story much credit. He tended to remain calm until his prey was in reach—like a lion, doing honor to his name.

"We've been expecting him. No need to worry, we're ready. You just stay back in the kitchen and I'll take care of the rest. I'm going to make sure Randy has the van ready to go to Sinatra's mansion."

"No."

"No, what?"

"No van, no Sinatra."

Before he was elected, Kennedy liked to stay at Sinatra's house when he was on the West Coast. Sinatra was a master at throwing discreet parties for select clientele with spectacular ladies and ungodly quantities of alcohol. But the singer was blacklisted now for his connection to Sam Giancana, the capo of the Chicago mafia and another regular at La Scala.

"The president's staying with Bing Crosby."

"Isn't Crosby a Republican? I wouldn't want to be the one to pass the news to Sinatra."

"That's not all. They're sending over a plane—to quote Lawford, 'So you can get there quicker.'"

"But it's just two hours by car to Palm Springs . . ."

"Plane and escort." Emilio shrugged.

In the kitchen, everyone rolled up their sleeves and got to work on the order. *"Don't skimp on the fettuccine!"* Peter Lawford had roared into the phone. "Plus salad, some beef, and a few bottles of wine. Everything better be perfect!"

Jean, Emilio, and the rest of the crew drove to the airport with a Secret Service escort on motorcycles from the presidential motorcade, lights flashing and sirens blaring all the way until they reached Air Force One. No one dared to utter a word.

Crosby's colonial mansion was in an isolated area far from the touristy parts of Palm Springs. The estate was large enough to satisfy the privacy needs of Kennedy, who came out to greet them when they arrived. After the necessary formalities, Emilio and his team went straight to the kitchen. The president, clearly tired from his obligations on that trip, invited Leon to partake in two of his most relaxing vices: a Havana cigar and a daiquiri. They sat down together on the glassed-in porch. Kennedy was wearing a black polo, white pants, and loafers. Informal and elegant. Leon, who never let his appearance slip, was in a jacket and silk tie, a button-down shirt and matching pocket cloth, and Italian loafers—and wore the same boyish smile as always.

"When I was a kid, I tried to make it into your country," the president said.

Jean was surprised—unpleasantly surprised. But obviously he couldn't hide the secret of his identity from someone who had the FBI, the CIA, and the Secret Service under his command.

"In the summer of 1937, I was in Biarritz, right by the Spanish border," he continued.

Leon couldn't believe it.

"In '37? You must have been a kid . . . ," Leon said. "What were you doing there in the middle of the war?"

"I was a kid, all right. I'd just turned twenty. It was my grand European tour while I was at Harvard. My father wanted information, too. He became the American ambassador in London later that year— I guess they'd been planning to give it to him for some time—and he needed a neutral outsider's perspective on where things were headed in Europe."

"Who better than his son, then?" Leon said, hovering somewhere between scandalized and alarmed.

"Exactly," the president responded, smiling. "We were in France, Italy, Germany. This was the dawn of fascism, and my father tasked me with interviewing the . . . let's say *the right people*."

Kennedy blew a diffuse smoke ring before continuing.

"My father was on Franco's side, but Roosevelt's government still supported the Republicans. And the reports he was getting were, to put it lightly, a little biased. His gut told him the war in Spain could be a powder keg that would lead to another world war, and he wasn't wrong," Kennedy admitted. "A lot of this ended up in my undergraduate thesis. You know, right through the forties, my father recommended that the US stay neutral in European conflicts and keep out of war no matter what—no military or financial support."

Leon listened, not daring to interrupt. Then, finally, the president looked him dead in the eyes.

"Did you fight in the war, Jean?"

"No. I was too young. But my father suffered the consequences."

"Your father and your older brother, right?"

"Yes."

"I lost my brother, too. Joe. He died in flight, on a mission in 1944. He was my friend, my hero."

Kennedy raised his glass, Jean followed suit, and they both tipped them back firmly, as though drinking down a hard-to-swallow memory.

"You must miss it, right?" Kennedy asked. "Your home."

"Sometimes, yeah . . . ," Jean conceded, frowning to express a measure of doubt. "But I left at a bad time, and it doesn't seem like the situation's changed too much. In Spain they still hunt you down if you dare to disagree with the government."

Their conversation about the political situation in Spain made Jean think of the talk he'd had the night before with his children. They were of an age when they could easily fall into a trap set by someone trying to wheedle information about their family out of them.

"Jean-Georges, Cécile, come here a second, Papa's got a treat for you," he'd said.

He had sat them down at the kitchen table and taken an ice-cream cone out of the freezer for each of them. He looked at his son and his little girl, her glimmering blond hair—*My God, it seems like yesterday Donna was pregnant, and already they're walking and talking*—and while they tore into their desserts, he told them a story about his name, one that had little to do with reality but that he believed would be effective.

"Do you know why we're called Leon?"

"Nooo!" they both replied.

"The origins of our name go back very far into the past, and they have to do with the king of the animals. The lion symbolizes strength, bravery, dignity, and constant struggle."

They listened to their father with gleaming, wide-open eyes.

"Those are things I needed to make it out of the country of our ancestors, where there were good and honorable men and women, but where I didn't feel like I could live my dreams. So I decided to come over to America, a land of opportunities for me and my children—for the two of you."

"How did you come here?" Jean-Georges asked.

"Papa took a ship and left France, the land of lions, to come to work in America. If they ever ask you where I'm from, if anyone wants to know where Papa's from, what should you say?"

And the kids shouted boisterously, in unison, with a smile:

"France! You came from France!"

"Very good! That's right! Good kids!" their father congratulated them, stroking their cheeks.

Leon had grinned, but deep down, he was ashamed. He didn't like having to lie to his children. He'd convinced himself that he was doing it for everyone's good. When they were older, he would tell them the truth. He hoped that when the time came, they would understand, and that they wouldn't reproach him for deceiving them. Leon took comfort in the thought that this white lie could save them lots of headaches.

"We'll have to continue our conversation another time, Mr. Leon," Kennedy said, bringing Leon's reminiscing to an end. He stood up and stretched out his hand.

The president's previously relaxed expression turned tense as walked back into the house. Jean followed him inside with his eyes. There, in a dimly lit room, half a dozen people were chatting and passing out drinks. Cigar smoke darkened the space where a figure had just arrived, one who seemed to shine with her own inner light. Jean watched Kennedy make a beeline to Marilyn Monroe, who took the president's arm.

The most powerful man in the world and the most sensual and longed-after woman treated each other with hypnotic familiarity. That weekend had been planned so the two lovers could be together.

Leon watched them with his trademark indifference. But there was also an envy that he would never acknowledge. How long had it been since he'd felt so close to Donna? Since they'd spoken to each other in soft voices, since they'd touched in a way that made their skin tingle? Since they'd been together because they wanted to, and not because they had to? They barely ever spoke now, not gently, anyway. They fought, and each time they pulled further away.

The same had been happening of late with JFK and Marilyn. Jean had sensed the distance growing between the president and the actress. It was like a curse with her—the same thing had happened with Sinatra. Her doomed affairs seemed to pile up like cast-off clothes in the bottom of a closet. Sinatra had dumped her. Arthur Miller had remarried and was waiting on a child, and Joe DiMaggio lived outside the limelight, struggling with his longing to return to the love of his life and the pathological jealousy he felt when other men made eyes at Marilyn.

Jean had seen her enchantments firsthand. Whenever she dropped in at La Scala, in the company of some hangers-on, not visibly drunk but too out of sorts to be coherent, Jean would drop his usual feigned aloofness and approach that lost but lovely woman with care.

One Saturday night soon afterward, someone called the restaurant asking for him.

"Jean?"

He was surprised to hear a woman's low, hesitant voice on the other end.

"Marilyn?" he guessed.

"Yes, Jean, it's me," the actress confirmed in a broken voice. "I'm calling to tell you I won't be in for dinner tonight. I'm a little tired. Could you send some dinner over for me, please?"

"Of course, you can count on it. Fettuccine and rosé?"

La Scala's customers made good use of its delivery services. Marilyn had grown used to calling in for a warm meal whenever she didn't feel strong enough to leave home.

"That's right."

"You'll have it in half an hour, OK?"

Marilyn sent him a kiss through the receiver and hung up.

Fettuccine Leon was La Scala's spin on a dish that had made it to Hollywood several decades before and had quickly become a classic. The now-ubiquitous Alfredo sauce, widely thought to be an Italian classic, was actually just an American adaptation of the *pasta in bianco* that millions of Italians ate at home. But since Douglas Fairbanks and Mary Pickford had brought back the recipe from Alfredo's restaurant in Rome after their honeymoon, local chefs had started adding an array of cheeses, butter, cream, bread crumbs, grilled chicken, cubed tomatoes—anything to give the dish their own personal touch. Marilyn liked it extra creamy, with lots of Parmesan and chopped beef, and it became another of the restaurant's fixtures.

First had come the mostaccioli Natalie, the rigatoni à la Debbie Reynolds, the grenadine of beef à la Paul Newman, and chicken à la Dean Martin. Then, when Marilyn took a liking to it, Jean Leon had renamed his fettuccine Leon in honor of the actress: fettuccine à la Marilyn.

Leon took the order to Marilyn's home himself. It wasn't his first time there. The actress lived in Brentwood at 12305 Fifth Helena Drive, close to Bel Air and not far from La Scala. It was a house on a narrow street, with iron bars over the windows and an interior she herself had decorated with knickknacks she'd brought back from Mexico—a country she loved, where her mother was from. As was her assistant, who lived in Marilyn's home with her and Pat Newcomb, Marilyn's secretary.

Jean remembered the first time he'd made a delivery to the actress. *Yes, please, the usual. Fettuccine and rosé.*

He'd rung the bell nervously, and Marilyn had taken her time opening the door. She'd answered with her eyes lowered and a glass of bourbon in her hand, wrapped in a pale-pink silk robe. Leon went into the dining room to set down her delivery, and she followed him in. She whispered, coquettish like a cat's meow, but there was something wounded in her voice, too.

"I met him a few years back at a party, at the home of this producer, Charlie Feldman," she began, as though they had been conversing for hours. Leon was confused but had a guess about who the actress might be referring to in her disordered monologue. "I was with Joe . . . He was so irresistibly handsome that I couldn't help but write my number down on a scrap of paper and leave it in his jacket pocket. He was a promising young senator at the time." She sighed and went on, then jumped ahead in the story. "We saw each other in the Malibu Cottage, at Pat and Peter's Palm Springs house, at the Beverly Hilton . . . at . . . so many places, Jean, places where Jack and I made love in secret, for years . . . years, Jean . . . and now . . ." She stopped to delicately dry her tears. "Now it's over, no calls, no meetings . . . Peter told me. Like that . . . without explanations, without anything. The same way he came into my life, all at once, he's up and written me off."

Jean didn't need to ask—he knew "Peter" meant Peter Lawford, the president's go-between.

"But I've still got his brother . . ."

"Bob?"

"Yeah, we've seen each other a few times lately," she admitted.

Marilyn got up to fill her glass.

"It all started at the birthday party. When Jack turned forty-five, at Madison Square Garden in New York." Marilyn recalled the day she had immortalized singing the most sensual "Happy Birthday" that had ever been heard. "Did you see me?"

"Why don't you put that drink down and have a bit of pasta?"

She paid him no mind, grabbing the bottle of bourbon and dumping out another healthy portion. She added more ice cubes and continued as though he hadn't said a word.

"I was the president's birthday present. I sang live in front of fifteen thousand people. Everyone in America was watching, even Jackie. With that dress, like a jeweled glove squeezing my body . . ." Marilyn ran her hands over her hips. Watching her, Leon could see why men found it hard to control themselves around her.

"You were a sight to see."

"Something happened that night that I could never have predicted."

"What?"

"When I got up from the stand after performing, I ran into his brother."

"Bob?"

"Yes, Bob, and I cornered him against a wall, and I would have showered him with kisses if Ethel hadn't been with him."

"You jumped on Bob Kennedy in front of his wife?"

"Yes, Jean, I was drunk, but I knew I'd have a better shot with the president's brother than with the president himself. Or maybe both at the same time . . . who knows." Under the sway of the alcohol, Marilyn Monroe was dreaming out loud in her dining room, and he was a witness to it. A partial and worried witness.

"Marilyn, listen to me and eat something," he said, offering her a plate of his fettuccine.

The actress pushed aside a lock of blond hair that had fallen in her eyes, went over, and gave him a kiss on the cheek.

"Your Donna is a very lucky woman."

"My Donna," he repeated softly, with some remorse.

"Thanks, Jean."

"Good night, Marilyn."

Two months later, nearly the same scene took place. Jean never knew what state she would be in, whether her mood would be glum or ecstatic.

"Jean! Hey! Come in," the actress greeted him, this time in a white satin robe.

"Hi, Marilyn, how are you?" Jean asked.

"Good, good . . . ," she said, a bit apathetic.

"Should I leave this in the kitchen?" Leon asked, not wanting to linger too long.

"Yes, please. I'll go get the money," Marilyn said, disappearing down a hall.

Leon walked through the dining room toward the kitchen. That was when he saw him.

"Hello, Jean."

"Hello, Bobby."

The brother of the president, the attorney general of the United States, Robert Kennedy, was pouring himself a whiskey. He looked relaxed; he had taken off his jacket and rolled up his shirtsleeves.

Jean knew that they had already seen each other the night before at La Scala. Robert had been sharing a table with Marilyn, Pat Newcomb, and Peter Lawford. Rumors of a relationship between Marilyn and JFK's brother had been floating around for some time, but Leon had ignored them and had kept his mouth shut.

"You want one?" Kennedy offered Jean the bottle of Jack Daniel's in his left hand, which showed his wedding ring.

"No can do, Bobby. I'm just here to drop off Marilyn's dinner. I've got to hurry back to the restaurant. We're full up tonight," he said, excusing himself. "I'm just doing this one delivery, because, well, you can't say no to Marilyn."

They exchanged a glance. The actress arrived and paid Jean, who left with an ambivalent feeling, a discomfort he couldn't shake.

He walked back to his car, breathing in the hot, dry air that came in from the Pacific coast and filled the night with the aroma of eucalyptus. It was harder and harder to recognize the Marilyn he had met years ago, the pre-Kennedy Marilyn. That joyful, curious, and unpredictable woman who had waltzed right into the kitchen to learn to make fresh pasta the way Emilio did it. The Marilyn who had captivated Jean Leon, who had chatted him up one night long ago, after accepting his invitation to a glass of wine at the famous chef's table.

"*Jean Leon.*" As he started the engine, he remembered the way Marilyn had pronounced his name that night, around closing time, with a provocative French intonation.

"Like the painter," he said, as he always did whenever someone tried to pin down where he was from.

"Gérôme!" she said exultantly. "*Je l'aime.*"

Jean was surprised she had heard of him.

"Have you seen the women he paints?" she asked. "When I look at them, I see my reflection in them, I swear it . . . Something about the sight of them is just wonderful."

She giggled, but then put her hand in front of her lips, while in his mind Jean reconstructed those scenes of slave markets, Turkish baths, and seraglios, like something from the *Arabian Nights*. It was true, Gérôme's women had a voluptuousness in their bodies identical to Marilyn's.

"You're right," he said. "Gérôme's women are very . . . stimulating."

He had loved that spontaneous Marilyn. She had real personality, even if very few people ever got to see it.

"You know I almost became a princess?" she told him one night when she was finishing dinner alone at table fourteen.

"On-screen or in real life?" Leon asked her.

After waving over a waiter and motioning for him to bring a glass so Jean could share the last bit of her champagne, she continued: "A real princess, with a prince, servants, and everything! Luckily it didn't work out."

Leon was intrigued by her story. And the actress loved telling it.

"It's a secret, but I can tell you because I know you'll never share it with anyone else."

"You can count on that."

"I could have been princess of Monaco."

"Really?"

"Yes, really, aren't you listening?" she said between giggles. "Aristotle Onassis was pushing for it. He had stock in the casino in Monte Carlo, and half of the principality was his. He wanted to bring back the splendor of the French Riviera, and he came up with this scheme with Gardner Cowles, the editor of *Look*, for Prince Rainier to marry a big Hollywood starlet . . ."

"No!" Jean responded, his mouth falling open as he leaned forward, desperate to know the rest.

"Yes, yes!" the actress replied. "Cowles proposed my name to Onassis. And so they offered it to me. I didn't know the first thing about Prince Rainier."

"So what happened?"

"Cowles and Onassis skipped over a very important detail . . ."

"What?"

"Rainier was already in love with a Hollywood starlet."

"Grace."

Those conversations, so sincere, so unexpected, never happened anymore. The cheer in Marilyn's face was gone—now it was ever more pallid and tortured.

On the drive back, Jean mulled over the scene he had just witnessed with Marilyn and RFK, and it kept eating at him even after he was back in the dining room overseeing the dinner rush. He gave everything his usual once-over, making sure there were no smudges on the wineglasses or silver, no dust on the bottles behind the bar. The headwaiter came over and informed him in a trembling voice that there was an especially high-priority guest there that Saturday.

"At table thirteen, sir."

"Sam Giancana?"

They had met a few years back through Frank Sinatra, and when Jean opened La Scala, Sam Giancana and other prominent Italian Americans started frequenting the place. At first, Leon didn't find anything unusual: "Momo" Giancana had been in La Scala many times, though he was more a fan of Puccini, the restaurant Frank Sinatra had since opened two streets away.

But then, when Jean thought more about it, it seemed like too much of a coincidence: only a few minutes earlier, he had greeted Bobby Kennedy, one of Giancana's sworn enemies. Sam wasn't pleased with the two Kennedy brothers. He'd put up a fortune to help get them into the White House. And now, from the attorney general's office, Bobby was starting a crusade against organized crime.

"Sam! Welcome! Good to see you!"

Leon greeted Giancana and his menacing companions. One of them, the slimmer, more serious of the two, stared him down, while the other made a grimace it was hard for Leon to ignore.

"Jean, my friend," the mafioso said with a smile, opening his arms in a sign of satisfaction, "it's not easy to find a place like yours, Jean, with good Italian cooking. You got one hell of a chef here."

Not a single trace of the spaghetti they had served the gangster remained on his plate. Just a few splotches of red and the crumbs from the bread he'd used to sop up the leftover tomato sauce until the plate was nearly spotless.

"Thanks, Sam, I'll tell Emilio—he'll be happy to hear that."

Later he learned the men with Giancana were two of his most feared enforcers: "Needles" Gianola and "Mugsy" Tortorella.

The next day was a Sunday, and Jean worked all day until very late. He closed up and went home, exhausted but satisfied. Everyone back at home was asleep.

The restaurant was closed on Mondays. That was their one day off a week, but even then, Jean liked to wake up early and drive over there to relax. He preferred to avoid the hustle and bustle of mornings at home while the kids were getting ready for school. He picked up the newspaper that the paperboy had left by the door, made a coffee in the kitchen, and glanced at the headline:

MARILYN MONROE FOUND DEAD

Impossible! He brought his hands to his head, pushing his hair back anxiously. *Marilyn.* He had just been with her. He had served her . . . yes. Her last supper.

It can't be, he repeated over and over. *It can't be true.*

He felt that same old jabbing pain in the pit of his stomach. His brother. Jimmy Dean. And now Marilyn Monroe. She'd never be back there at table fourteen, she'd never greet him at her house in her robe, she'd never enjoy his fettuccine again, she'd never tell those incredible stories or share her intense, bewildered thoughts.

He felt something crack inside him. For the first time in ages, he missed his wife.

CHAPTER 11

Donna barely ever set foot in La Scala nowadays. But one day, La Scala came to her.

"Special home delivery. I've got lunch for you."

"Emilio?" Donna opened the door for him, surprised.

In a chance conversation with Jean, Emilio Nuñez had learned that Donna hadn't left the house for two weeks. She was laid up sick with a fever. Jean had told him everything was under control, that the children were at his sister-in-law's house, and he was shocked when the cook hushed him with a cutting remark. Emilio had headed over to the house within the hour.

"You look like hell . . . ," Emilio told her as soon as he saw her, his forehead creased with concern.

"Don't come too close, I'm worried I'm contagious."

"God forbid Jean should get stuck without his head chef."

They both laughed. Emilio went straight to the kitchen to unwrap the food. He told Donna to take it easy and sit down, that he would take care of everything.

"It's been a long time since you've eaten at La Scala, it's not like the old days. You're lucky: I've made you *caldo gallego*. It's my mother's recipe, it'll do you right."

He hadn't even begun to heat it up when they heard the sound of the keys opening the front door. It was Jean. He acted like nothing was out of the ordinary, but to Donna and Emilio he was an open book. They were the only two people who always knew what he was thinking.

"We're backed up bad in the kitchen, Emilio."

"I'm busy here."

Jean stared at him with a clenched jaw, not blinking. "I can take care of this."

And, against all predictions, Jean kept his word. He served his wife dinner, then waited for her to fall asleep so he could go to his sister-in-law's house to collect the children. He called out sick the rest of that week and took care of his family. Donna couldn't remember a single time he had stayed at home when La Scala was up and running.

"I know I'm losing an important part of their lives, Donna, but I want to leave something behind for them, and right now is when I need to really take care of it if I want it to turn into something big."

"Jean," she said, "listen, your children being happy now is just as important as their future, if not more so."

"I know, Donna, and they are happy," he responded, convinced.

"Are you sure?"

"I think so. I mean, nobody can have everything," Jean said, shrugging.

"Oh, that's obvious. But we have a choice about what we give up. And as far as I can tell, you're happy to lose your wife and kids—all for the sake of your restaurant," she hissed.

"You and the kids are the ones I'm doing all this for."

"No, Jean, no, we're not," she said, indignant. "Be honest enough to admit that everything you do, you do for you and nobody else. You've barely finished one thing before you start thinking about another. What's next? A new restaurant, an addition to the one you have, buying a winery to make your own wine? Isn't that your latest idea? Don't use us as an excuse, you don't even believe yourself. The important thing is always you and your projects and your stars and your bigwigs . . . Where do we fit in, Jean? *Where do I fit in?*"

After all the time that she had been with him, the unconditional support she had offered, after putting aside her own goals . . . she found herself relegated to second place. Just like when she had wanted to be an actress. But Donna didn't want to cry, not in front of him. She was tired of crying.

Monday came, and Jean Leon returned to La Scala.

Donna, now recovered, resumed her own life, taking care of the kids.

They saw little of each other over the coming days, as if they were punishing each other for something that had broken during her convalescence.

"I've been doing the numbers, and . . ."

Jean sat down next to his wife, who had been stretched out on the sofa reading a long book. She closed it with an evident lack of enthusiasm. She was expecting the usual monologue about how the restaurant was running, and she didn't care. But Jean, to the surprise of both of them, wanted to fix things.

"Next year will be our tenth anniversary." Donna raised her eyebrows. "And we never did get around to taking our honeymoon."

"But Jean, what—"

"You feel like going to Rome?"

Donna didn't say yes right away, but she also didn't want to overthink it, to doubt him, or to look for ulterior motives. That offer, coming out of the blue, made her think for a moment that maybe they could go back to the beginning, to where they had started from. But then the story came out—*why* they'd be going to Rome. No surprise, it was about the restaurant, not about their relationship.

As Donna knew, La Scala's famous delivery service, which she herself had enjoyed when Emilio had dropped in unannounced, had been a success beyond all expectations, and it had led to the most far-fetched orders over the years. In February 1961, for example, when a request came through during the filming of *Cleopatra* in London.

Liz Taylor had just started acting again after a bout of pneumonia, and she was making even tougher demands than usual. One day, she got a craving for cannelloni. But not just any cannelloni, no. Neither the hotel where she was staying nor any other in London could match the cannelloni Lolita with grilled beef and white truffle béchamel, her favorite dish at La Scala. It was named after the novel by Nabokov, in homage to the friendship between Jean Leon and James Mason, a fervent fan of those cannelloni and the star of the film based on the book, which Stanley Kubrick was directing.

Donna knew the story of Liz Taylor's favorite cannelloni. Jean himself had told it in a moment of weakness, making Donna suspect that her husband might feel something more than mere professional loyalty for the actress. He was a seducer, and he'd also let himself be seduced. Donna had realized it the previous winter, when she'd seen the efforts he made to get those cannelloni to Liz Taylor at the Savoy hotel in London. Those were the actions of a person who couldn't say no. Luckily, Emilio had come up with a solution. It turned out the best option for getting the cannelloni from LA to London in a still-edible state was to ship them off in a plane in a temperature-controlled package with dry ice. Done and done.

When she saw that miracle waiting for her on the table, Liz Taylor, pleased as punch, ordered another round for the next day.

"Now she wants to say thanks, so she's invited us to Rome, where she's filming the final scenes of *Cleopatra* at the Cinecittà studios."

Donna's first reaction was to put him in his place and say no. She didn't trust him. She felt there was something behind all this . . .

"I want to go back to Europe, and I want to do it with you."

In the end, Donna finally relented. And so Jean Leon and Donna Morgan started packing for their first big trip together after nine years of marriage. Though she wasn't entirely happy about it, Donna agreed to leave the children with her sister for the duration of the trip. They knew they needed to be alone and far away from everything. After a long time in the City of Angels, they would now enjoy the romance of the Eternal City together.

"I'd like to visit the cellars in Monte Testaccio in Rome with you," Jean said on the airplane after they'd taken off. "More and more, I feel like I want to make my wine in Europe."

"In Italy?"

"I haven't decided. But not here, anyway, not in California. I've been thinking it over, and I have a few European locations in mind. The first one I want to consider is this area near Rome. And I want you by my side . . ." He looked at her warmly with a smile on his lips. "Like when we were just getting started at La Scala. What did we use to say before, when we first knew we had luck on our side?"

It's a sign, Donna remembered.

After they'd spent hours monotonously contemplating the ocean, a voice came over the intercom to say they were flying over the Iberian Peninsula and informed them of the time remaining until their arrival in Rome.

"Look, Donna," Jean murmured, leaning into his wife and pointing out the window. "That's my country."

"This is France?"

"No. Spain. We'll probably fly over Barcelona. That's where my family is."

Donna stared at him, as if trying to make out the letters of an unknown language. *Spain?* The roar of the airplane engines was suddenly overwhelming. Her ears were ringing, it was hard to breathe, and she wanted to vomit—and not from the cabin pressure or from airsickness. The person sitting next to her was, suddenly, a perfect stranger. They were thousands of feet in the air, and she understood nothing.

"I know I should have told you before, but . . . Donna. My name is Ceferino Carrión. We've still got two hours until we land. Let me explain it to you, please."

Donna missed the view of Rome from the air, as well as the panoramic sights of the Colosseum, the Forum, and the Vatican from the taxi. She was distracted as she watched their luggage getting hauled up to their hotel room, as she listened to the high-pitched voice of the concierge, as she stared at the enormous pastoral painting hanging over the head of the bed. She still didn't completely grasp what a *fugitive from military justice* was, let alone what it meant to have seven brothers- and sisters-in-law with their own families that she had never met or even heard of.

"So you've never been in touch with them?"

"Not since my sister's wedding. That was . . . in September of 1950."

"Twelve years," Donna said, stunned.

"Twelve years," he repeated.

It wasn't easy to keep talking. She was in a state of shock. Of bewilderment. Of incredulity. *Cefe* what? *Spanish? I have a mother-in-law, brothers- and sisters-in-law, nieces and nephews.*

"You have to call them. You have to talk to your family," she said. This much she knew.

CHAPTER 12

"Hello?"

Leon recognized the voice on the other end and got so excited, he didn't know how to continue. He had been in the same situation before. But back then, it had only been a year since his family had heard from him. Now it had been twelve.

"Hello?" the voice insisted. "Who is it? Who's speaking?"

"It's me. Who is this?" The only thing that occurred to Jean was to resort to the insolence of his youth.

"It's Mari! But you . . . no, it can't be."

"Mari! It's Cefe!"

His sister's cries came through the telephone so loudly, even Donna, herself excited, could hear them. Jean managed to hold back the tears, but not the laughter, even as a pit of uncertainties opened for his wife.

"What about Mama?" he asked timidly.

"Yes, Cefe. She's alive! Everyone else, too."

The prodigal son expelled all the air he'd been holding in since before the conversation began. Donna sat next to him on the bed and put her arm around him.

"I'm in Rome right now. I'll call back tonight. Can you try to put Mama on? I'd like to talk to her—and to you all, too."

All Mari could do was repeat how pleased she was to hear his voice again. They still had a little time to run through what had happened in their lives over the years. Jean told her he was married and had two kids, looking affectionately at his wife, who followed the conversation with the same feeling of warmth. Even though it was in Spanish, Donna didn't need to know the words, just as, hours later, she would intuit everything he said when he spoke with his mother.

But it was hard for her to follow along with the welcome-home festivities the entire Carrión family staged for them in the Estación de Francia one week later. A mother-in-law, lots of brothers- and sisters-in-law, and a countless number of nieces and nephews who didn't even wait for the couple to get out of the train car to hug them, kiss them, and shout in jubilation on being reunited with their beloved Cefe. They went to the Hotel Ritz to eat. Jean had reserved a room there for the two days they would stay in Barcelona. During lunch, he patiently responded to all the random questions that his family, especially his sisters, hurled at him across the table. Jean answered and translated some of the conversation to Donna. No one in his family spoke any English.

Toward the end of the meal, he stepped away for a smoke, and then came the long-postponed conversation with Ana María—Chiqui, his little sister, the one he had always been closest with. She was the one who knew him best, and she wanted the most answers. He knew she had suffered from his inexplicable absence. But he was also dying to tell her about all he had achieved, and how well life had turned out for him.

"Mama prayed a mass for you every day for all these years, ever since the day you left. We thought you had died!" his sister reproached him, but then she bombarded him with questions: "Could you not have called? Or sent a letter? Some news? Anything? Why did you go? Just to live another life, a new life?"

Chiqui didn't believe that song and dance about how their father's and brother's deaths had left him broken, unable to deal with the responsibilities bearing down on him . . . How he would never satisfy the expectations placed on him . . . How he was still on the run from the military.

"It's been hard for us, too," she said to him.

"I'm sure it has, Chiqui. Believe me, I am. But—"

"And all that was years ago, Cefe, nobody remembers your military service now," she said, trying to reassure her brother.

"The whole time—"

"I know, Cefe. I missed you, too. We all did."

They hugged, then dropped their seriousness and solemnity. They returned to the table, smiling and relaxed, to join everyone else. Jean tried to catch up with all his siblings at once. They were all married, they all had children.

"Seems we don't know how to keep the Carrión boys around," his sister said with a roll of her eyes.

"What do you mean?" Jean asked.

"Don't exaggerate," Paco said to her, then addressed his brother directly. "I didn't cross the pond, I just took a job nearby, in Vilafranca del Penedès. It's not much more than thirty miles from here."

"In Penedès?" Jean exclaimed.

He couldn't stop laughing and clapping his brother on the back. Another stroke of luck.

"Tomorrow we're going to my brother's house in Penedès," Jean told his wife when they returned to their room, bringing that special day to a close. "And I've got a very good feeling about it."

When Jean had made his list of possible vineyard sites a year before, he had settled on a half dozen regions between Italy and Spain. Penedès was one that Dr. Maynard Andrew Amerine, a professor of enology at UC Davis, had marked out for special consideration.

"I don't recommend California. Not Napa or Sonoma Valley. If you want to do something different, look to Southern Europe. First of all, the land will cost you a fourth as much. You should get your vines from France, but I wouldn't plant my vineyard or make my wine there."

Maynard was eminent, a reference point for winemakers from all over the world. And he loved visiting La Scala. A man of the world, classy and elegant as an English lord, he was distinguished but not stiff—rather the opposite. He was an affable talker and always jovial. He loved being around people and, as he confessed to Leon, he had a strange hobby: sighting the rich and famous. He was fascinated by the local royalty who gathered at La Scala. Nowhere else could he rub elbows with the celebrities he admired so.

Maynard sang the praises of the food, but especially of the extensive collection of wines in the cellar. Leon had started with the classics: first-growth Bordeaux, Grand Cru Burgundy, Mumm, Dom Pérignon. But his curiosity was inexhaustible, he had money to spend, and soon he was buying cases of Vega Sicilia from Spain, Biondi Santi from Tuscany, old vintages of Colares and Madeira from Portugal.

He had heard rumors about a new generation of major players there in California looking to change the wine industry and go head to head with Old Europe: the Mondavi brothers, Robert and Peter; a young Croatian, Mike Grgich; Richard Graff, who had recently purchased the Chalone vineyard. Jean wanted to know about these men—what they were doing, how they were doing it, and—just maybe—whether he could get in on the game.

Wine exists to give pleasure. So when you drink it, you should have a good time. The professor repeated that maxim to Jean so often, Jean made it his own. And he decided to share with the professor the idea that had been circling around in his head for some time. Jean had consulted with wine professionals, but he'd never had an expert in his inner circle, and he couldn't let slip the opportunity to ask for his advice.

"Everything as it should be, Dr. Amerine?"

The man was finishing his linguine with clams and his glass of zinfandel, a robust red made from a grape brought to California during the

Gold Rush. The varietal was experiencing a wave of enthusiasm, with wineries like Ridge and Mondavi producing excellent examples. Leon was well aware of the professor's love of those wines, so different from the Primitivo wines of southern Italy, although the grape was allegedly the same.

"What's it look like to you, Jean?" Amerine answered, gesturing to his near-empty plate.

"You want a coffee or a digestif to finish off?" the host asked him, as he knew Amerine never had dessert.

"Well, if you're buying, I'll have another coffee. If you'll join me, that is," the professor responded gratefully.

Leon waved down one of the bartenders, then sat next to the professor.

"It's strange," Jean said, "but I've noticed an American will pay six hundred dollars for a wine that doesn't match the food and isn't even up to the quality you'd expect for that price."

"It's epidemic in restaurants. But why should you care? Your wines are excellent, your recommendations are always on the mark, and in the end, if they want to fork over that kind of money, who are you to stop them?"

"I appreciate your kind words, Professor. It means a lot, especially coming from you. But that's not for me, selling other people's wines, no matter how good they are or how much money I can make."

"What do you mean?"

"I want to have an exclusive wine, something you can't get anywhere else, high quality, a perfect match for food. And I've decided to make it myself."

"Are you sure?"

"One hundred percent. I've thought it over, and I'm ready."

Dr. Amerine nodded, already interested in the project and hoping to make his own small contribution.

"You're a brave man, my friend. But let me tell you something, Jean. With wine, it's one thing to recognize quality; it's a whole other thing to achieve it."

"My idea, and you can tell me what you think, is to compete with the French. And for that, I need to get a small vineyard with low yields. If I could do that, I'm sure I could make waves. I don't want to just buy something and let other people run it, I want to oversee it myself, down to the last detail, like an artisan."

Jean described his strategy, which was based on two concepts: quality and prestige. That was nothing new; he used the same approach at La Scala, and it had served him well. Why not use those same principles to make his own wines?

"Am I crazy?" Leon asked him.

"Mark Twain said a person with a new idea is a crank until that idea succeeds!" Amerine said boisterously. "Not only do I like your plan, I'd be more than willing to lend a hand."

The specialist's support and advice were critical to helping Jean learn what he needed to know. Before leaving for Italy, Jean had made notes on the potential locations that most interested him, making use of the information the enologist had given him. One of the names the doctor had mentioned intrigued him more than the others.

"El Penedès. An unjustly overlooked area, with excellent soil conditions and climate." On the way to his brother's house, Jean looked back over the notes he had taken on Penedès during his conversations with Amerine.

Optimal climatic conditions, with a microclimate similar to the best valleys in California. Altitude, proximity to the sea, and soil composition make it an ideal place for grape growing.

In the times of Julius Caesar, the wines of Penedès were famous in Roman banquets and throughout Europe. Millions of amphoras from the area were sent by sea from Tarragona to the capital of the empire.

Observations: Try new varieties. Plant red and white varieties, and don't limit yourself to macabeo, ull de llebre, garnatxa, and malvasia, which are the grapes the locals make their wines with.

I've got a good feeling, Jean had told himself when he saw, on top of a hill some eight hundred feet above sea level, an old vineyard stretching out over clay soil, rocky, chalky, on a plot of around one hundred fifty-seven hectares—fifty-seven wooded, the other hundred arable. Only eighty were under cultivation, in the hands of a pair of tenant farmers with one mule and one goat.

And then, on October 12, 1962, that good feeling materialized when he purchased Mas d'en Rovira in Torrelavit for 6 million pesetas. It was a common-sense choice, not one of Jean's typical irrational impulses. Amerine cast the deciding vote. Before Jean bought the property, he'd sent some soil samples to UC Davis for analysis, to determine whether the varieties they hoped to plant would thrive in that soil. Once they'd gotten the green light, Jean Leon bought the land. They had put down 275,000 pesetas as a deposit, and now he was paying the remainder, and the property would be his.

But not his alone.

Spanish law didn't allow foreigners to own more than twenty hectares of land, so, because of the size of the estate, Jean decided to register himself as the owner of the ancient home on the property and put everything else in the name of his brother, Paco, who lived in Vilafranca.

Having his brother, Paco, there was a blessing and a curse: Jean needed him to purchase the land, but it meant placing his trust in a greenhorn, someone who had never seen a farm up close, knew not the first thing about soil, and had no idea how the wine business worked. Fortunately he wouldn't be alone; Jaume Rovira, a young winemaker who had studied enology in Madrid, would be there to support him.

Jean would be able to follow the progress of the winery from the US and would only need to go to Penedès a few times a year.

The day after buying Mas d'en Rovira, Jean Leon got up very early to take a walk around his estate. Jaume was surprised to see him climbing the hill toward the vines. He left what he was doing to come out, greet him, and take him on a stroll through the property.

Rovira was pleased to show Jean the distribution of the vines, the different varieties, and to take him into the heart of the vineyard. This was the place he would begin planting the strains of white and red grapes they'd decided on over the phone. Jaume was excited to put Jean's suggestions into practice. Jean didn't have much experience with wine on the production side, but his plans for Penedès were clear-sighted and revolutionary.

Rovira reached into the vine shoots, the long, thin branches emerging from the trunk. He fingered one of the tendrils and then pulled off a cluster. Attached to a broad leaf was a shoot with a cluster of juicy berries, their pulp sweet, their skin yellow.

"They look like pearls!" Jean Leon gawked, stroking them delicately with his thin white fingers.

Rovira knelt down, and Leon followed suit. The enologist dug his hands into the earth and grabbed a handful of soil, letting it slip through his fingers.

"These are poor soils," Rovira said.

"Are you saying the land isn't good?"

"Quite the opposite," Rovira said reassuringly. "Like the farmers say, when the soil is rich and fertile, you plant vegetables. When it's less so, you plant wheat or garlic. But when the soil looks like it has nothing left to offer, that's when you plant your vineyard."

The two men walked up a path to a small, templelike shed piled high with tools, fabric, bags, and other items belonging to the young enologist. There, they took shelter from the sun, which was falling at an angle, sitting on the stone bench under the barely protruding roof of the shack. Rovira served them two glasses of wine from a pitcher.

"I don't know what anyone else has told you," he said, gesturing across the surrounding fields, "but we have promising conditions here, and soil that can make a magnificent wine. Of course, we've got to have patience. You can't rush the vines."

"With persistence and a little luck, I'm sure we can make it happen," Jean Leon replied, excited by this new horizon before him. "There's no doubt about it, you look at the world differently with a little wine in your stomach. And this one isn't bad at all."

"Trust me, ours will be better!" Jaume assured him.

"Good enough that people won't just drink it, they'll talk about it, too. I'm sure of it!"

Jean Leon raised his glass in a sign of optimism, wishing the young man well. But instead of toasting, Jaume grew thoughtful.

"Actually, people here are already talking about it."

"Why do you make that face, Jaume?" Leon asked with a touch of concern.

The enologist didn't move a muscle. He was concentrating. He watched the ripples on the surface of his wine, and with them, the sediment settling into the bottom of the glass.

"A sediment of hatred and rancor . . . ," Rovira murmured.

"What do you mean?" Leon asked, knitting his brows.

"These objections, they're leaving a sediment of hatred and rancor," he repeated bluntly, looking Leon in the eyes.

"Objections?"

"So to speak. The farmers, some are raising a stink," Rovira said. "A lot of them don't agree with what we're trying to do here."

Leon felt great respect for the local winemakers, but he was going to do things his way, whether his neighbors and their laborers liked it or not. And he had Rovira's education and experience with the land to help bring tradition and innovation together.

Over the next several months, during the growing season, Rovira drew on every technique he knew to achieve good results. He scattered ash and oil on the vines so that, during pruning, the ash would fall into the clefts and protect the vines from frost. In the depths of winter—again, to avoid frost damage—he would spread manure across different parts of the vineyard, letting the steam from it radiate over the plants.

These were ancient methods that had been handed down from generation to generation. Jaume had learned them from the people who lived on the land, and he wasn't one to look down his nose at tradition. At the same time, he had studied enology in Madrid, he knew the science behind his work, and there were times when his ideas struck the neighboring farmers as madness. He thinned his crops mercilessly in the pursuit of better juice. Many treated the harvest like an act of fate and let the fields sit untouched for much of the year, but Jaume spent every waking hour in the vineyard, inspecting the soil, the fruit, the leaves. He was just a kid: when he met Jean, he hadn't finished his degree, hadn't done his year in the army, and had just gotten his feet wet at Can Nadal, a cava winery. But he was determined to make Mas d'en Rovira, which the new owner had dubbed Château Leon, the most sophisticated winery Spain had ever seen.

CHAPTER 13

When the summer of 1963 came, Jaume reminded Leon's brother, Paco Carrión, of all the work that had to be done before harvest: plowing, digging, tilling, mulching, cleaning the trenches, culling, pulling up vines, pruning, training the vines, replanting, grafting, sulfur treatments, scattering manure . . .

"All this work in the fields means hiring day laborers."

Rovira knew some he could trust: Tomàs from Ca l'Alió; Cisco "the runner," who would use his cart for anyone who would hire him; Delfí Finet from Cal Marçal, who plowed with his goat; and Sadurní from Ca la Nàsia. Outsiders came in for the harvest in September, including a group from Sant Pere de Riudebitlles. The neighboring farmers often worked for each other, and had their own system for calculating work hours: a day's use of an animal and a plow, for example, was worth the same as three men's shifts. A shift meant seven pesetas for a man and five for a woman, but Leon paid ten per shift for all. Still, not even the extra wages could bring in all the workers they needed. The paper mill in the Anoia basin was up and running now; they paid even better, and many of the farmers were more than happy to give up the vineyards for work indoors. The future didn't lie with the land.

To make matters worse, Paco Carrión was still adapting to his responsibilities. He didn't have a good head for the business; it overwhelmed him. And he spent money like crazy, despite Jaume Rovira's warnings. Since there weren't enough hands for the job, Paco decided to buy a tractor.

"Did you talk it over with your brother?" Rovira asked him, mistrust in his voice.

"What do you think?"

"What I think is eight hundred thousand pesetas is a lot of money!"

"I know, but this isn't just some toy, we need it!" Paco answered with irritation.

"Fine, fine. You know best! Do what you want!"

"My brother is the only one who needs to know, and I already told him," Paco said, enraged. "He thought it was a good idea and said he'll send a money order to the office of our lawyer, Micaló."

Despite the distance, Paco and Jean spoke on the phone often, especially about money. Jean had always trusted his brother with the money, but things were now about to change.

"Jean, it's me, Paco . . ." Paco sounded like a man at a funeral.

"Hey, Paco! What's up? Everything good at the château?"

"I'm calling about the money for the tractor . . ."

"It didn't get there? They told me it would arrive in less than a week!"

"Oh, no, no, Jean, don't worry. The money got here . . . But the lawyer took it and . . ."

"What, Paco? What happened?"

"Well, he blew it all on a poker game," he said.

"What?" screamed Jean on the other line. "Goddamn it, Paco!"

"I'm sorry, I'm sorry. It's my fault. I never should have trusted that guy."

"Did you know he was a gambler?"

"No, I didn't," Paco said.

"Shit, Paco." Jean took a deep breath. Losing his temper at his brother wouldn't bring the money back. "Well, don't beat yourself up over it. What happened to you could happen to anyone. You trusted a man of the law. Now it turns out he's more rotten than Emilio's teeth. What can you do?"

"I'm sorry, Jean, I really am," Paco said. "I promise you I'll go get it myself this time, and I'll keep it under my mattress until it's time to pay the vendor."

"I know. But you can't do anything about it now, it's over. It's just money, it's not the end of the world."

Leon tried to cheer his brother up, but he knew it was time for a change. The best thing would be to put Jaume Rovira in charge of the château and cut Paco out of any responsibility. Especially if he hoped to make the kind of wine he was aiming for, one with personality and character.

His vineyard already reflected the fruits of tradition and change. But this moment was also a turning point in Jean Leon's project of making a true estate wine, one that could compete with the French châteaux, where the provenance of the grape could be traced back to the vineyard. If he succeeded, he would be a pioneer of estate wines in Spain.

Leon and Rovira wanted to acquire vine cuttings from the best wineries in France. They called at the doors of the high temples of wine: red grapes from Château Lafite Rothschild and Château La Lagune in Bordeaux, white from the vineyards of Corton-Charlemagne in Burgundy. They bought thirty thousand vines of cabernet sauvignon, cabernet franc, chardonnay, and merlot, plus a small quantity of pinot noir.

But the French saw Jean Leon's interest in their goods as a threat, and what they sold him was practically unusable: withered vines that produced insipid fruit. By the time Leon and Rovira realized, it was too late to complain. Instead of balking, they stuck to their wits, returning to the vineyards after pruning season, when they found the winemakers' leftover cuttings piled up like garbage next to the walls separating the vineyards from the roads. Jean and Jaume loaded two vans with the vine shoots. They worked at night, filling their sacks by the light of the moon, and before they vanished over the horizon, they agreed to take two separate routes, just in case one of them got caught.

Jaume Rovira passed over the border at La Jonquera without problems. Jean Leon, who entered via Hendaye, had a brush with the civil guard. Two agents in tricorne hats and trench coats motioned for him to halt, and Leon stopped and rolled down the window.

"Good evening, sir." They gave him their habitual military salute.

"Good evening," Leon replied laconically.

"Where are you coming from at this hour?"

"From Bordeaux. From the Médoc, close to the Gironne. In Bordeaux," he repeated, his nerves getting the better of him.

"Bordeaux. You don't have to tell us twice. You mind showing us what you're hauling back there?"

Leon agreed. He got out of the van, opened the back doors, and lifted up the sackcloth. Seeing all the cuttings, the civil guards looked at each other with surprise.

"What's this about?" they asked with suspicion. "What are you going to do with all those branches? I don't think you can bring those into Spain."

Nothing about this looked right. And Jean had to make up an answer quick.

"Do you gentlemen have kids?"

"Yes, why?" both guards responded in unison.

"Because this wood I have here is used to make candy."

"Candy?!"

"That's what I said." Leon gestured at the shoots and buds. "We have a little factory close to Barcelona. We make candy there. You know how licorice is made from a plant root? Well, other flavors of candy are made that way, too."

The agents glanced at each other and nodded, convinced by the explanation. Once more, they gave a military salute and stepped away from the border to let the van through. Leon swallowed and exhaled. It wasn't until many miles later that his fear dissipated—not until he reached the estate and saw that Jaume had made it across with his haul as well.

They planted the new varieties right away. Leon and Rovira oversaw the entire process. They had high expectations, but they knew it was a gamble. First, despite all the advice Leon's contacts in the US had given him, no one could truly say what would happen until the fruit was fermenting in the vats. The vines wouldn't yield any for three years—maybe even longer, depending on the weather. And Jean and Jaume agreed they wouldn't settle for just any fruit—they had high hopes for their first bottling, and they wouldn't bring their wine to market unless they were convinced it was perfect.

They brought in workers from Sant Pere de Riudebitlles, and there were no complaints from the tenant farmers, most of whom were happy to lease out their land and go to the paper factory in Anoia. The new workers were easygoing, and that meant Jean and Jaume could follow their instincts and plant the foreign varieties there without anyone raising too many difficulties. They seemed to have finally won the farmers over to their side. Leon agreed to pay the workers double the price for the first harvest. Everyone was happy with the excellent conditions offered by the American, as they called him in Penedès.

Everyone except for a few holdouts who didn't like the outsider's new ideas. Pulling up all the traditional varieties was an irritation—or worse, an insult. There were grumblings, day after day, in the old café that had once been the lavish headquarters of the local agricultural cooperative, with its brick facade, its six Ionic columns, its cornice decorated with two large globes, and its eye-catching stained-glass windows.

A pine bar, varnished hundreds of times, greeted its motley clientele: backwoodsmen, veterinarians, travelers, and salesmen who would order their coffee, wine, or brandy at the bar or play cards at the tables with wrought-iron legs and marble tops. In the wintertime, they filled the stove with hazelnut shells and it warmed the whole room as the smoke from cheap cigars mingled with the toasty scent of the nutshells. In summertime, the customers cooled off in the rear courtyard, beneath the shadows of an old pergola, and the open windows and doors let the breezes pass through.

"Sometimes you just can't wrap your head around what these goddamn foreigners are after!"

"He wants to make a different kind of wine."

"Different?"

"Yeah, with grapes from another country. He's planting them now."

"That won't bring anything but trouble."

"So?"

"I hope lightning strikes that goddamn foreigner!"

These curses and ill will didn't take long to reach the gates of Château Leon, and they would cause far more damage than the recent hailstorm that had wrecked the vineyards. One foggy afternoon in 1963, a single intermittent point of light shone through the darkness of the vineyards. Shadows swathed the silhouette of a man in a cape who was trying to make a spark catch by striking two stones against the dry, squalid brush next to the wall separating the vines from the woods. After a couple of failed attempts, hitting his fingers and cursing, he finally succeeded.

The fire leapt up and consumed the bushes, the underbrush, the tree branches. It spread in flickers, and with it came the unmistakable odor of combustion. It tore through the woods and surrounded the vineyard, insatiable. The trunks of the pines and holly oaks were defenseless without their needles, branches, and leaves to gird them against the oncoming menace. When night fell, the fire redoubled its fury, goaded on by the wind. The vines turned to embers. The tenant farmers and neighbors ran out to save them, but there was nothing they could do. The next day, the dance of colors and sulfurous vapors vanished beneath the sunlight. And nothing was left but smoke and ashes.

In Torrelavit and the surrounding villages, everyone talked about it. People regretted what had happened, and many pitched in to help clear out the land. In the afternoon, with the fire extinguished and the smoke cleared away, Jean walked to the highest point of his estate to contemplate the charred, desolate landscape in silence. The fire had made the temperature sweltering, but Jean couldn't help shivering with dread. His mind returned to the days of his childhood.

It was impossible not to recall the flames that had ravaged his home in Santander. That had been a tragedy for his family. They could have died. But they managed to pull ahead that time, and he was determined to do the same again. It would take more than a fire to make him give up on his dreams.

They still had cuttings they could plant. And Jean wasn't alone: he had his brother and Jaume Rovira, not to mention his own innate capacity to rise again—this time, literally—from the ashes. He would be the phoenix of Torrelavit.

One night at the end of November, just months after the fire, the phone rang. The first ring was long. That meant the call was coming from afar, from overseas. America.

"Jean, it's me, Emilio."

He was surprised to hear the chef from La Scala calling him at that hour. It was almost midnight in Spain.

"Something terrible's happened, Jean." His voice was cracking. "They shot the president. Kennedy's dead!"

CHAPTER 14

Jean followed the aftermath of John Fitzgerald Kennedy's assassination and funeral through the badly informed Spanish press. In his own private, discreet way, he felt the desolation he imagined sweeping over America. Donna sounded dismayed on the phone, but the renovations and decoration work on the enormous new house the couple had bought after returning from their trip to Europe kept her busy. Still, her impatience with her husband was growing uncontrollable.

"Do you not get it, Jean? Once again, I'm the one who has to take charge of all the family's business. You told me this would be our home, that we would share the responsibilities, you and me, that everything would be done to our liking. It had to be this big so we could invite family and friends over for the weekend, and all of us could spend more time together . . . And now here I am, feeling claustrophobic and alone, and I have no idea how to fill up all this space . . ." Jean was no longer sure whether his wife's phrases were trailing off because she was angry with him or just depressed. "Where are you now, when you're supposed to be here deciding how we're going to arrange things?"

"What do you think? That I wanted the fire to happen? That I burned up my own property so I wouldn't have to be with you?"

"Of course not."

Donna sighed, and it was obvious their conversation was going in circles.

"Stop letting everything eat at you," Jean said. "Things are coming back together here. There's a lot to do, but I'll be back home by Christmas at the latest, and then we can celebrate together."

He did, as promised, make it back to California before Christmas. But, of course, a Christmas celebration in the home of Jean Leon meant Donna had to share her husband with the guests at La Scala with their endless lunches, dinners, and take-out orders. And the nights stretched on into morning, with the owner's blessing and participation. It was like clockwork: the more Jean's wife wanted him home, the more he fled from his responsibilities to her and to his children.

He wouldn't allow anyone to talk to him about what was going on. Not his few close friends, not even his Spanish family when he returned to see the improvements they'd made to the vineyard. When they asked about his wife and kids, he fell silent. No one dared get in the middle.

Except for Emilio.

"Can I be honest with you?" he asked Jean.

"Please. Shoot. If you didn't, you wouldn't be you."

"Right. But are you going to listen?"

Jean took a sip of wine and lit a cigarette, pretending to give his friend his full attention.

"For a long time now, you've been out of it, and I'm afraid you're about to screw things up big."

"You're not going to bring up the Newport thing again, are you? For every project of mine that turns out badly, I've got a dozen guaranteed successes. Newport is old news."

Emilio didn't believe that Jean had really gotten over the failure of the restaurant he had opened in Newport Beach. It had been Dick Powell's idea: the actor had told him he should expand the business, opening a spot on that touristy part of the shore just an hour by car from La Scala. But it had turned out badly, and Jean reacted as he always had when faced with failure: he wouldn't admit he'd been wrong, and he wouldn't listen to reason.

Emilio, who knew the business as well as he did, quickly figured out their mistake. The places that did well in Newport Beach focused on seafood, and in an Italian restaurant like La Scala, the seafood was mainly there to round out the menu. To Emilio, Jean had been arrogant and had gotten ahead of himself, whereas Jean felt it had just been a slipup, that he should have gotten to know the market better and not put all his trust in Powell. He'd learned from it, he said, and he wouldn't make the same mistake when he sought to expand the business in the future.

"That's the problem. You've got a million projects in your head, and you're dead set on all of them no matter what."

"You know me, every day brings a new idea . . ."

"Is the vineyard not enough?" Emilio pushed harder. "Look at all the time you're spending now to get a winery up and running on the other side of the world. You haven't even finished that and you're already on to the next thing. Why don't you focus your energies on taking care of the things you have, maintaining them, maybe even enjoying them?"

Jean listened with a glum face. But Emilio knew one thing that would break through his studied indifference.

"Yeah," Emilio added, "it's no wonder you're destroying your marriage and your family."

Emilio had expected a reaction, and he got one: Jean was now giving him his undivided attention.

"While you go on adding to this myth you've built up, flaunting this idea you have of yourself as a visionary, you're hurting the people who love you the most."

Jean took a deep breath and downed his glass of wine in one swig.

"You're right. Maybe I shouldn't have gotten married, let alone had kids. I was in love, and I thought a wife and kids were what I needed to feel complete and happy, to feel like I'd made it. But all that came before La Scala."

"Jean, for God's sake, how can you say that?" Emilio couldn't believe his ears. "Do I need to remind you how hard Donna worked in this kitchen and this dining room to make them what they are today? Do I need to remind you how proud you were when Jean-Georges and Cécile, your little princess, were born? Get it together, man! Who are you trying to fool?"

"You've got it, Emilio. I'm just a goddamn egomaniac, and I don't think about anyone but myself."

"You promised you'd listen. So let me talk, and then you can do whatever you feel like," he admonished him harshly. Jean opened another bottle, not bothering to look at the label. "You act like all that matters is you and your projects. Not to mention the women who come and go or the waitresses you butter up and then a month later they're gone. Well, I hate to tell you this, but you're not alone. You have a family, like it or not, and they're a part of you."

They stayed there, neither uttering another word. As the silence persisted, Emilio gathered the papers scattered over the table: seasonal menu proposals they'd been trying for days to sort through before making a final decision.

Sitting next to him, Jean sipped deeply from his glass of wine. His eyes were pinned to the floor. He had already been through one recent failure, and he wasn't ready to bear another, deeper, more permanent one. He had so much to take care of. He needed to reorient his priorities . . . reduce expenses.

The restaurant had shown Jean that he could make his dreams come true. And now he had a new dream that was taking shape, that was on course, and that no one would stop: his wine, with his name on it, made in his country . . .

"I can't make any promises," Jean said quietly.

"You don't have to promise *me* anything." Emilio shook his head, disappointed.

They turned back to deciding on the menu. They had spent the spring trying to update La Scala's cuisine to keep their clientele on its toes—not only the old faithfuls, but those new faces that were constantly renewing Hollywood, the ones whose names Jean wasn't always able to recall.

The main dishes would soon include a salad with radicchio—a bitter-tasting vegetable, a kind of chicory—imported from Treviso in the Veneto. The radicchio, they'd found, paired brilliantly with white beans and clams. They were also considering another dish destined to become a La Scala classic: a rabbit cacciatore. Emilio could make it like no one else. First he grilled the meat, then he mixed it with just a touch of red and green peppers and served it with a whiff of olive on a bed of angel-hair pasta.

The two men spent several days talking over each item, readying a menu that would make its debut at the beginning of summer. They knew that to stay on top, to keep the stars coming in, they would need to adapt and change.

And sure enough, the stars kept coming. Despite the failure of their Newport Beach experiment, Leon's relationship with Dick Powell was cordial as ever. A few months earlier, NBC had canceled Powell's show, but the actor and host kept dining at La Scala after he left the company's Burbank studios. He still hung around with actors and celebrities, he wasn't going to let those ties slip, and he had a great nose for sniffing out opportunity. Especially when it came to politics. Those were fraught times, politically, in America. The country hadn't yet awakened from the nightmare of Kennedy's death, and Democrats and Republicans were both gunning for the presidency.

One night, Powell reserved a table for four. Jean remembered the story Powell had told him about the night of Richard Nixon's defeat in the California gubernatorial race back in 1962. Powell had tried to comfort Nixon and had recommended he support a young candidate to jump in and replace him. Jean remembered it because he knew that young man's name—he'd even shared a drink with him some time before. And he was just as happy to see him again when Powell brought the man and his wife in as guests, along with his own wife, the actress June Allyson, for a double date.

It had been years since Jean Leon had seen Ronald Reagan.

"You did it, kid." Ronnie greeted him with open arms that seemed to embrace the entire restaurant. "Jimmy would have been so happy. The place is beautiful!"

"I'm so glad you're finally seeing La Scala."

The ex-actor, since transformed into a politician, introduced his wife, the actor Nancy Davis, and Jean showed the group to their table. Reagan excused himself for a moment to catch up with the owner privately and reminisce about a moment they'd shared with Jimmy.

"How's your new career going?" Jean asked.

"Good, I can't complain. You know they fired me from *General Electric Theater* because they said my monologues were too political, and it was no longer convenient for the company to keep me on the air. You know what I say? Great!" he declared. "I don't like being censored. I'm getting my footing in the party. Powell, George Murphy, and William Holden are helping me."

"You were already headed in that direction. I'm happy for you, Ronnie."

"You're not doing so bad yourself."

"Fact is, I'm about to make one of those dreams that came up in our conversation that night a reality . . . Do you remember?"

"The wine?" Reagan asked.

"Damn, Ronnie! You've got some memory!" Jean shook his head admiringly. "If everything goes right, in a few years La Scala will be serving the best food *and* the best wine in the city. Maybe you'll be governor of California by then and we'll be able to toast our achievements."

Years passed, and Jean and Emilio were happy: the menu went on growing and changing, and the restaurant remained a success. But over time, they spoke less and less to each other one on one—and one day, in one of those unexpected decisions of his, Jean took off, leaving everything in Emilio's hands for weeks on end.

It was September 1969. Harvest time. The owner of Château Leon—only those closest to him knew he had adopted that name for the winery—arrived in time to take part, along with his wife and his children. It had been seven years since Jean had bought the vineyard and planted the first vines, but so far, something had always gone wrong— the crop was too thin or they'd had late frosts, or hail had ravaged the vineyard. One way or another, it wasn't up to their standards. This year was different, and it was time to make the wine a reality. To mark the occasion, the children would visit their father's homeland for the first time.

The kids spent part of the airplane trip asking their father about their relatives. Jean, with uncharacteristic patience, tried to describe each of his siblings, and if memory failed him, he invented what he couldn't recall. The children were hopping up and down with excitement when they entered the main hall of the Hotel Ritz, where Jean Leon was to reunite with his family. His children would soon understand why their mother had warned them about the strong hugs and countless kisses they would receive.

The harvest, the high point of the grape-growing cycle, had turned into a huge party, and every household invited family and friends up to take part. The sun was hot and the air muggy, and all the workers were dripping sweat. Carefully but firmly they would push aside the leaves to pick the first bunches. With little more than a precise flick of the wrist, they would use their knives to cut the shoots with their clusters, and the grapes would fall into a basket or pail until it was full. Then the workers would take the grapes back to the main building for pressing, carrying the precious fruit in their arms or else loading it on the back of a mule.

Jean walked over to his wife, smiling, and whispered into her ear. "Get ready for something you've never seen or even imagined."

They left the children with their cousins, Paco's kids, and Jean winked at Jaume Rovira.

They walked down the stairs to the cellar, where the stones around them seemed to breathe out moisture. They were guided by the smell of the grapes in the vats, about to turn into must.

"Once you throw the grapes into the vat, you have to stomp them with your bare feet so the wine gets enough color and strength—that gives it body and aroma."

"I hope my feet are clean," Donna added with a laugh.

"I'm sure they're fine. May I?" Jean knelt down to take off her sneakers.

"Thanks. Very kind of you," she whispered playfully.

Donna rolled her thin blue jeans up over her knees, then hopped from the floor up to the footrest. From there, she gathered her strength to jump inside the cylindrical vat, which was fitted with ropes over the top to hold on to. The ropes kept the person inside from slipping and also helped them push with all their force to press out the juice.

Once inside, sunken up to her knees, Donna cracked up laughing, almost like a child. Jean loved seeing his wife there like that, smiling and shrieking with joy. Her legs, those beautiful white legs, were submerged in that mess, the sweet scent of which gathered in his nostrils. No matter what she did, the juice splashed all over her clothes. Her jeans were ruined, but what did it matter?

Donna held on to the edge of the vat, afraid of falling. But she couldn't stop laughing. She was having a blast, that much was clear. She turned around and around, still leaning on the wall, and when she felt safer, she let herself go. Keeping her eyes on her husband, Donna took two steps out into the middle of the vat, let down her hair from its ponytail, and started dancing. Jean nodded, as if giving permission to this momentary ballerina. He paused for a moment, imagining himself savoring a wine with Donna's flavor.

Delicately, Donna continued to crush the grapes, stepping over and into and around them, moving her feet gracefully. Jean stopped hesitating: he took off his sneakers, jumped in, and landed in the middle of the grape clusters, which felt like a soft cushion under his feet.

"Let yourself go," she whispered in his ear.

Jean realized that Donna was shivering. They grabbed each other's shoulders, hugged, and, following tradition, turned in a circle, stomping on the grapes and squeezing them out with vigor, letting the juice run out under their feet. The aromas they released made the couple want to come closer, touch each other, be free. They moved in the same rhythm. Their hands explored each other's bodies. A moan rose up and vanished. It was a mirage that evoked old memories and swept them aside for the times to come.

Their bodies weren't the same ones as in Las Vegas all those years ago, and their relationship had soured since then. But there, surrounded by the perfume of the grapes they were crushing, they cut loose, and for a moment, they were once more those kids full of dreams who had an entire future to build together in front of them. It was a magic moment, intense, charged with memories and hopes for Donna and with feelings of peace, fullness, and satisfaction for Jean. The moment bore sweet fruit, but soon enough, Jean had forgotten it, in thrall to another of his schemes.

Jean had now spent seven years traveling back and forth to Penedès at harvest time and Holy Week, with just two thoughts in his head. It wasn't only the wine he was obsessed with, it was also the memory of his long-lost but much-beloved Catalan cuisine, the food he remembered from his childhood. Both were equally important to him, and he wanted to bring both back to the tables at La Scala.

In mid-May, after the season had ended, he and Jaume were invited to Valls for a *calçotada*, an event that finally allowed Jean to bring both those affinities together. Valls was the capital of this decades-old Catalan tradition: a festival centered on grilling *calçots*—the region's long, thick green onions—and eating them with plenty of roasted meat, sausage, and white beans. Now Jean could rediscover his country's gastronomy, this time with a professional's eye. It would also be a dress rehearsal for the wines of Château Leon: they had bottled a barrel of their first vintage especially for the occasion.

"Our wine—do you think it's good enough for a *calçotada*?" Jean asked Jaume nervously. "I know we're not quite there yet."

"Yeah, but it's a way of maintaining a tradition that will bring goodwill to our winery. In the old days, when the people from Camp de Tarragona invited you to a *calçotada*, the cava producers from Penedès used to take advantage of it to promote their wines," Rovira explained. "It's good business, and they know you're a somebody in Hollywood . . . Besides, we can't miss it. The star guest will be Salvador Dalí."

Leon remembered a conversation he'd had about Dalí not even a month before—a conversation with Alfred Hitchcock, who was a regular guest at La Scala.

Hitchcock went to La Scala because he was crazy about their ice creams and their quiche lorraine, but mostly because he was addicted to a cocktail he would later dub the mimosa. It was very sweet, with a base of champagne, sugar, and orange juice. The drink was his weakness, and Jean knew it. As soon as he saw the director come into the restaurant, Jean already had the bartender making one.

"Thanks, Jean! You're spoiling me. You know who got me drinking these, right?"

"No."

"Salvador Dalí," he said.

"Dalí, the painter?" Leon exclaimed, surprised.

"Yes! The genius! I've been drinking them for more than twenty years now. I had my first one back in 1945, when we settled on our terms and signed a contract to collaborate. We were going to toast with champagne, we had it ready to go, but then Dalí had one of his moments of inspiration. Fifteen minutes later, we were sealing our agreement with mimosas."

Hitchcock had gone on to explain to a rapt Jean Leon that Dalí had made the cocktail there in Hitchcock's office, mixing the champagne they had brought for the occasion with a pitcher of orange juice from the coffee table and a few sugar cubes. To say Hitchcock had taken a liking to it would be an understatement. For twenty years, it was all he had drunk with his meals.

When they arrived for the *calçotada*, Rovira and Jean went directly to Masia Bou, an ancient farmhouse that had been converted to a restaurant where the festival would take place. Leon looked at the *calçot* shoots about to go in the fire. They were long and thin, ideal for grilling. The tables were set with bowls full of *romesco*, a dipping sauce of hazelnut, almond, roasted garlic, grilled bread, oil, and peppers. Waiters set up grills for the sausage and lamb. Boxes of oranges waited patiently to be called to the stage for dessert. Jaume brought out the cases of Château Leon so the servers could pass out the bottles.

They were going over the last details when they saw Dalí arrive with his retinue—with the mayor of the town, Romà Galimany, at the head. Jean was surprised to encounter a Dalí not at all like the eccentric personage he had seen on TV. This man was distinguished and elegant, with his unmistakable mustache and its twisted tips.

Dalí walked slowly, conversing with a girl who accompanied him, holding on to his arm. She looked like an actress: blond, with round cheeks and sassy lips. She stared up with devotion at the genius in his suit jacket and black suede pants. Only one note of color broke the artist's somber image: a red necktie. His hair was long, combed back, with sideburns that descended to his jawline. Mayor Galimany introduced them and did the honors while they all shook hands. When Dalí heard Leon was the owner of La Scala, he raised his eyebrows and squeezed Leon's hand even tighter.

"A pleasure!" he said with a slightly husky voice. "That's the restaurant of the stars, right? I've heard excellent things about it."

"Thank you, Mr. Dalí. Whenever you're in Hollywood, you're invited!"

"Much obliged!" the painter responded, raising his cane toward the sky. "I'll keep that in mind, though I don't often make it to those parts!"

Jean was surprised by all the bracelets of different shapes and colors that Dalí wore on both wrists. At least six per arm. The hand that wasn't holding the cane made a reverent gesture to the right so that Leon would look at the tall, slender girl who was leaning slightly on the artist's forearm.

"I present to you my muse, my inspiration: Miss Amanda Lear."

The girl smiled and stretched out her hand for Leon to kiss it.

"A pleasure!"

At that moment, the owner of the farmhouse, Mr. Gatell, came out. He was scrupulously groomed and very elegant, and he held a medal in his hand. His intention was to give it to the artist, conferring on him the status of *Calçotaire Major Honorari de Catalunya*. In front of all the invitees, Dalí submissively bowed his head to receive it. Of course, he couldn't show the medallion off during the *calçotada*, because immediately afterward they put a bib on him to protect his suit when he dipped the onions in their sauce. Bibs were passed out to the other guests as well, and pile after pile of *calçots* began to emerge from the fire, served on the traditional roofing tiles.

"You'll forgive me if I don't try your wine," Dalí said to Leon. "I don't have the palate for it. I'm more of a cocktail and vermouth man. I do have my ideas about wine, though. It always seems to me that the person who really knows it doesn't drink much, but enjoys it, savoring it slowly and penetrating its soft secrets."

Speaking of secrets: one that Dalí didn't often confess to in public, in order to avoid rousing the ire of all the other Catalan restaurant professionals, was his special liking for the restaurant Reno in Barcelona.

The emblematic white awning that stretched out over the corner of Carrer Tuset and Travessera de Gràcia had been greeting Reno's select clientele for many years. It didn't look like it, but beneath the shelter of that white canvas, countless deals had been settled and contracts signed. Afterward, the high rollers would celebrate inside, toasting with wine or champagne.

Jean had tried exquisite dishes there, extraordinary and original combinations he would later describe to Emilio. His obsessions were the salmon *kulebyaka* and the *poularde Demidoff.* He also loved other local restaurants, too, like Via Veneto (for its variety and elegance) and Botafumeiro, with its warm wood interior and silver chargers of fresh seafood, as wide as the waiters were tall. Leon wanted the menu at La Scala to remain unpredictable and intriguing, fusing the styles of those three gastronomic temples.

One day during his trip, Jean escaped to Reno to order the famous quenelles of sole. The dish was reminiscent of croquettes—little spheres of chopped fish molded with a teaspoon and bound with egg white and cream. At Reno, with its evident French influence, they were to die for. At the end of his meal, Jean couldn't help himself: he stopped the owner of the restaurant, Antoni Julià, who was walking through the dining room just then.

"Is everything up to your standards, Jean?" Julià asked with a smile and a touch of concern.

"Antoni, these quenelles are extraordinary." He pointed at his plate, where not even a crumb was left.

"Thanks, Jean, thank you very much. I'll tell the kitchen you said so."

"I'd like to ask you a favor."

"You name it. Anything for you!"

"I want the recipe for this dish. I want to take it back to America and offer it to my guests in Hollywood."

"My goodness. Jean, it would be a pleasure, an honor, even, for you to take one of my dishes to Hollywood." He asked permission to sit down. "But I should tell you a secret."

Leon leaned in toward him and sharpened his ears, not wanting to miss a single detail.

"The best quenelles, like these, aren't made with sole, even though we tell the guests that. We make them with trout or pike."

"We might have a problem, then. I don't know if pike like this make it all the way down to California!"

Both restaurateurs broke out laughing.

Before saying goodbye to the American, Antoni Julià gave him the recipe on a piece of paper, writing it out by hand. Jean was leaving Spain with a treasure that would soon grace his menu. And that menu, the one that would inaugurate the 1970s, would soon feature his own wine.

By now, Jean Leon was spending more time in Penedès than in Los Angeles. He had adapted to the slow, tranquil rhythm the country demanded, far from the frenzy and furor of Hollywood. Before, he'd lived among the stars, but now he was passing hour after hour on the ground. He had learned to bend his life to the pulse of the soil, to a different tempo: how to plant, how to care for the vines, how to watch them grow, how to learn from the leaves, to listen to nature. Unrushed.

But there, too, were factors he couldn't predict or control. Like the weather. He knew this, but he couldn't accept it, and every September he agonized over whether they would have a good harvest. All the signs had been right, though, in 1969: after seven years of grafting, planting, trying, and trying again with different grapes—pinot noir, chardonnay, cabernet franc, cabernet sauvignon—everything promised they would finally have the wine they were looking for. And now, in 1973, it was ready to drink.

Jaume Rovira ordered the first cases of the 1969 to be sent to Jean Leon back at La Scala. Rovira had split the vineyards into four parcels and had christened each with a name that had a story behind it—Jean Leon's story. La Scala Vineyard, for the restaurant that had opened in 1956 and had paved the way to success: eight hectares of cabernet sauvignon. Le Havre Vineyard, in memory of the French port where Jean had set off in 1949 in search of a new life: nineteen hectares of cabernet franc and cabernet sauvignon. There were ten hectares of chardonnay, divided into two parts: Cécile Vineyard, dedicated to his daughter and the apple of his eye, and Vineyard 3055, named for his taxi license number, in memory of the time when he had learned to choose his own destination while driving others to theirs.

From that well-drained yellowish-brown soil in La Scala Vineyard, cleared of stones, nearly a thousand feet above sea level, came twenty-two barrels of 1969 Jean Leon Cabernet Sauvignon. The pioneer vintage—the best and most inspiring one to date.

"This is a reserve wine, age-worthy," Jean explained to Emilio, just as Jaume had told him. "A wine for people who know how to savor the years of waiting, the years the wine has lived through, until the moment when the cork comes out and the glass is filled and brought up to the drinker's nose, and he takes a long sip, letting the flavor soak in as it goes down his throat."

"A reserve wine?" the chef asked him.

"*Reserve* means it's meant to be aged. Not many wines get that kind of treatment. A red like this needs two years in French oak and two years in bottle. After release, you can drink it or cellar it, and it will have a long life in the bottle."

Leon knew because Rovira had told him as much. Following the precedent of many great wines of Bordeaux, and increasingly those of California, Leon and Rovira made their wine with 85 percent cabernet sauvignon and 15 percent cabernet franc. They were chasing the same dream: for Jean Leon to achieve fame with a great Spanish wine from Penedès, one that could outshine the wines of Rioja. This meant they would follow the example of Rioja wineries, designating three levels of wine: *crianza*, *reserva*, and *gran reserva*. Each was aged differently, with different occasions in mind. The crianza was easy, accessible, a wine to be drunk every day; the reserva was denser and more dignified, meant to be savored and appreciated; while the gran reserva was the highest expression of what the soil of Penedès could produce.

They carefully looked after every single detail, even the label, which was sober and elegant. On the top, the name of the wine in red capital letters—*Jean Leon*—in a dignified, easy-to-read typeface. Underneath, in the center, to attract the eyes, was a drawing of the Château Leon estate. You could see a shapely vine row and, in the back, the house itself. Underneath this image was the name of the grape variety, also in red capital letters: *Cabernet Sauvignon*. In black were the words *Produce of Spain*, and then the year in red. The names of the designated growing region of Penedès and the specific subzone, Pla del Panadés, were at the bottom. Rounding off the trademark design were the bottle number and the signature of Jean Leon. This, he felt, was the calling card for his incomparable wine.

Jean reserved for himself the privilege of opening the first bottle of his wine at La Scala. He was surrounded by members of his team from the kitchen and the dining room, with Emilio Nuñez by his side, standing back to let Jean take center stage. Donna wasn't there. She hadn't been told.

Jean Leon staged the entire ceremony, and after the obligatory toast, he let everyone try it. They drank down several bottles. When it seemed he could leave, he shut himself up in his office alone, taking his glass with him. He hadn't dared to taste it until this introspective moment arrived. Later he would present his wine to the West Coast gastronomes, with the prestigious Professor Amerine in tow; soon enough, he would be talking about it to the wine journals and sommeliers. There would be time to feed his myth, his ego.

First, he needed a moment to savor all he had accomplished, allow himself a moment of introspection, of pride. But for some reason, he didn't feel any. It was as if he had a bottomless pit inside: the more he accomplished, the less content he felt. And since Jean didn't care to look backward, he couldn't discern the cause of his dissatisfaction. It never occurred to him that it might be his fault. He'd started out with a vision, but with time, it had grown blurry. He was moving from one project to the next without really knowing why. There was a mystery around his past, his roots, his achievements. So now what?

Who was he? Jean, the imposter?

Ceferino, the opportunist?

Again he had that feeling of being no one, from nowhere.

The more he saw his family in Catalonia, and the more time he spent in the vineyard, the more he longed to go back there. But from his day-to-day life in mythical Hollywood, Spain looked backward and frightening, and he recalled the claustrophobic feeling that had made him run away the first time.

What was undeniable was that Jean Leon was so far away from that Ceferino Carrión who was born in Santander and had fled Barcelona that he didn't even recognize him anymore—if there was still anything left of that kid who got so excited over every new project, every dream, and gave it his all until he had made it come true. That Cefe who had come to America ready to take the world by storm was still there in his willingness to undertake any adventure, in his unflappable will to make his name in the world. And, he had to admit it, in his need to be loved and recognized by the people he admired, the people he had looked to, as if into a mirror, when he had built up his own personality from scratch.

His thoughts turned to Jean, the new man he had fashioned in the USA with pride and resilience, and then he started to get a glimpse of what he wanted. He'd never confessed it to anyone, but when he thought back over his life, Jean Leon had to admit that on the path to success, he had sacrificed what most people considered the most important things: First of all, his family—not only his immediate family, Donna and the kids, but also those farther away, like his mother and siblings in Barcelona, whom he didn't speak to for so long. And he had given up those pastimes, like art and music, which had been so important to him when he'd lived in France. He had never thanked those anonymous people who had helped him out in his hardest times and whom he'd forgotten once he was surrounded by stars. He had dedicated himself to getting ahead by hook or by crook. Could he do it now? How? When? Why?

There had to be something between Ceferino and Jean, some middle point that represented who he truly was . . . *That,* he said to himself all at once, as though opening his eyes to something he had long set aside, *is where I need to look. The center. I need to find the center.*

CHAPTER 15

Jean had announced the news a few days earlier, over dinner with his family, to everyone's surprise. The California Restaurant Association had just named Jean president; the sitting president, Mike Romanoff, had decided to give up the post. It was a great honor for Jean to take the baton from one of the most illustrious figures in the world of haute cuisine. A new stage in the consecration of his name—his legend—and one more motive to stay away from day-to-day life at home, to his wife's dismay.

"Now that I'm president, we can use this conference coming up as an excuse to take the family to San Juan."

Jean-Georges and Cécile were over the moon. Donna was tired of playing the bad cop, but she also couldn't stand Jean blithely interrupting the daily routines she struggled to establish at home. But then, she would give in to any of his ideas if it meant the family could spend time together, for her children's sake if not for her own.

And as much as she hated to admit it, the best times she'd spent with Jean had been thanks to this kind of proposal from out of the blue. Jean knew that. And Donna knew that he knew it, and that he used that knowledge to his advantage.

"We'll have fun. We'll spend the whole weekend there. All I have to do is go to a couple of meetings, and the rest of the time we can spend together. We'll go to the beach, visit the city." Jean looked at his kids, who seemed up for it. "There's a famous castle there with a fortress. They still have cannons from the pirate ships that attacked the city."

It was a beautiful promise . . . but could he keep it?

San Juan greeted them with a tropical storm, sending down brief but intense bursts of rain. It leveled off quickly, and soon the hot sun was threatening to burn their pale skin, even in the shade. The post-storm heat was stifling.

The next morning, when Jean went to the first of his meetings, there was not a single cloud in the sky. Their hotel, the Miramar, faced the Atlantic and offered every luxury and comfort, so Donna and the children stayed close by to enjoy playing and relaxing by the pool. They had lunch at the buffet, which featured a wide selection of dishes the Leon family had trouble pronouncing. At dusk, they walked through the old town for ice cream and soft drinks. As soon as they arrived at the restaurant where they had agreed to meet for dinner, a waiter came over with a telephone connected to a very long cord before Donna could even ask for a table.

"Excuse me, ma'am, there's a call for you."

"For me?"

"Mrs. Donna Leon, right? Your husband is on the line."

"Donna, babe . . ." Jean's voice sounded distant. "I was trying to get ahold of you before. I'm so sorry, but—"

"You won't be here for dinner, either," Donna interrupted him.

It wasn't a question. It was an affirmation. And all the ill feelings that she had tried to suppress during the day she'd spent alone with the kids rose up in the form of boundless indignation.

She hung up and handed the phone back to the waiter.

Jean stood there, phone in hand, cut off in the middle of his explanation. Then again, he wouldn't have known how to explain to her where he was going anyway.

To do so, he'd have tell her what had been in his mind those past few weeks, the dissatisfaction that had tormented him and that he couldn't admit to anyone. Least of all to her. He'd have had to go back even further, to two or three months ago—or, if he were honest with himself, if he listened to his memory, even longer. All the way back to an unexpected visit over a year ago that had knocked some ancient memories loose.

It had taken place one morning while Leon was having his coffee at a table in the restaurant, reading a story in the newspaper about the Vietnam War. In the ashtray, his cigarette was burning down, untouched. The lunch shift hadn't yet begun.

"Jean?"

A man in dark-blue stovepipe pants, a camel coat, and worn-out loafers with no socks patted him softly on the back. A huge smile crossed Jean's face, and he stood up to embrace him.

"I can't believe it! Julio!" He wondered if his eyes were deceiving him. He hadn't seen his cousin in decades.

"Cefe! Excuse me—I mean, Monsieur Jean Leon . . ."

His cousin hugged him tight. Time had passed for Julio, too. His hair was whiter; he had more wrinkles and a bigger belly, but the same grin, the same energy, the same contagious vitality. The glimmer in his eyes had not faded in the least.

"You know how it is. I'm married now, and I'm on my honeymoon. I couldn't miss my chance to salute the king of Beverly Hills." Julio winked at him, just as he used to do. "So I dropped in. I wanted to surprise you."

He had done that, all right. But he wouldn't stay and eat, no matter how much Jean insisted. It had been just a brief hello, for nostalgia's sake. Julio had to be on his way.

"How is Uncle Ramón?" Jean asked.

"Papa died. Last year. He was all heart, and in the end, it was his heart that gave out on him."

I'm too late, Jean thought. He had been putting off a visit to his family in New York, and now . . .

"He used to show me clippings from the newspaper about you," Julio said. "He was so proud of all you'd accomplished. He always talked about taking a trip here to come see you."

Too late, Jean—Cefe—repeated to himself.

"Who could have imagined that Sinatra, the guy you and I saw together at the movie theater with Eva María, would end up being . . . a friend of yours?"

"Ah, man, I wouldn't exaggerate . . . ," he replied, recalling for a moment that night the four of them had shared at the cinema so many years ago.

He especially remembered Eva María. He had never called her like he'd promised. In fact, he had never contacted her again. But in the bottom drawer of his desk, he still kept a box with his amulet, his *cemí.* That little triangle-shaped angel she had given him to protect him during the voyage of no return from New York to LA.

"Whatever happened to Eva María?"

"She married the owner of the tailor's shop where she worked. They expanded the business, left the neighborhood, and opened a store in midtown. Her mom left not long after. You remember Mrs. Buenavida?"

How could he forget her? María Buenavida. That short, cheerful, nurturing, lively woman. So generous. He still owed her.

"She went to live with her daughter?"

"No. From what I heard, she went back to her country."

To Puerto Rico. San Juan. To Old San Juan, in the historic center of the capital.

"Calle San José, number 109," Leon said to the taxi driver.

Through the car window, he observed that part of the city with its blue paving stones and colorful buildings from the Spanish colonial period. *I can't overwhelm Donna with another hidden episode from my past.* The taxi traveled down the avenue named for the first governor, Ponce de León, parallel to the streetcar packed with tourists.

We can't survive another one of these delayed confessions.

In the distance, immaculate and imposing, rose the church of Saint Augustine. They passed in front of it, headed into the heart of Puerta de Tierra, the working-class neighborhood.

I don't have the heart to explain anything else to her right now.

And after driving over the narrow, cobblestoned streets, they reached his destination.

I don't even really know what it is I came to do.

Leon had the taxi stop in front of a building with a patched facade, with wooden railings and shutters and an inner courtyard bathed with sunlight. Some of the balconies were in deplorable shape; others needed a new coat of varnish as soon as possible. The decaying air of the place depressed him, and soon his apprehension was making him question why he had come. The sound of water gurgling in a fountain in the middle of the courtyard struck him as a good sign. The music he now heard was another, as were the lyrics.

> *Don't live for tomorrow*
> *forget your pride*
> *turn your back on your sorrow*
> *and your dreams will arrive.*

Salsa music was playing inside the building, and those words followed Jean inside like an omen. It was the memory of Little Puerto Rico that had brightened his days in the Bronx, dancing and eating with the Buenavida family at their joyful, raucous gatherings.

He grabbed the chipped wooden handrail, which creaked under his grasp as he walked up to the second landing. At the end of a small hallway was a door painted a garish green. He stopped in front of it and knocked. He cleared his throat and gathered his courage. Now there was no going back.

The door opened with a grinding of the hinges, and in front of him a woman appeared, so old that he briefly hesitated.

"Good afternoon," he greeted her with his best smile. "I'm sorry, is this the Buenavida residence?"

The woman brought her hand to her lips.

"It can't be . . . It's you!" She leapt into his arms while she repeated, "It's you! It's you! Blessed Mary, it's you!"

She pulled away for a moment to look him up and down, still not letting her powerful grip loosen, and as she stared, trying to believe what she was seeing, she exclaimed:

"Ceferino, it's me, I'm María Buenavida!"

Jean could see that life had mistreated her. The wrinkles had eaten mercilessly into her face, making it a map of hardship. Every one of those furrows was a testament to the time that had passed; every fold was a sign, a trace of pain, of hard work, of anguish, of the penury she'd had to endure.

It had been nearly twenty-five years.

"María!"

They hugged again, and the woman invited him inside. The dining room was almost bare. On the sideboard was a kind of altar with candles; in another corner, an image of the Virgin, a table with a transistor radio, and a two-seater sofa of brown imitation leather. Mrs. Buenavida told him to sit down while she smiled and caressed him.

"Ramón kept us up to date on all that was going on with you. I'm happy to see life has been so good to you."

There in front of her he stood, the very image of the Hollywood playboy. Elegant as could be, in a pin-striped suit and a white cotton shirt that emphasized the healthy color of his skin. His face showed the passage of time, his worries, but he also wore a winning smile. The kind she would have liked to see on her own son's face. Jean wanted to say,

I see it's been good to you, too, but there was no point in lying, it would be discourteous.

"Are you here to meet him?"

"Who?"

"Justo Ramón."

Without giving him time to react, María Buenavida explained that when her mother had died, she'd decided to go back home to take care of her son. A knot started forming in Leon's throat. It had never occurred to him that her son might still be alive.

"Come with me," María said to him. And once they were partway down a poorly lit hallway, she added, "Go ahead. Justo Ramón, look who's here to see us."

Immobile from the neck down, laid out in bed, was a man Jean's same age. He bore an extraordinary resemblance to him, though his frame was slighter. Like a photographic negative—a version of Jean dealt a harsh blow by fate. Jean felt a chill run up and down his spine. A part of him pulled away, telling him to run without looking back, but another part made him stay there to hear the other man out.

"You're just like I imagined." Justo Ramón's voice, unlike his body, was full of life and determination.

Imagine. That was all he could do. Jean wondered what it must be like to simply imagine life, from inside the four walls of that bedroom papered over with surreal floral motifs. He felt a paralyzing claustrophobia that reminded him of his voyage in the hold of the *Liberté*. But also of his present. This claustrophobia that had been hounding him a long time, but he didn't want to admit it to himself, because it had only one solution.

He shivered and stopped imagining.

The ten minutes he had allotted himself for the sake of politeness passed while he nodded, recollecting moments from his days in the Bronx—and, above all, avoiding the reminders of Christ whichever way he turned: there was a crucifix over the bed, another on the nightstand, a cross stamped into the cover of a Bible, and another on a biography of Saint Augustine.

"I hope you don't mind my asking, but . . . why did you come here?" Justo Ramón asked.

"Honestly, I don't know." Jean tried to work out a response. "I felt I owed something . . . to your mother, to you . . ."

"No! Not at all!" María Buenavida waved him off.

"I don't think of myself as a generous person. Not in the Christian sense." He pointed to the crucifix and the books on the nightstand. "If I'm honest, I've always put myself before others. And I doubt I can change much at this point. But I promised myself that one day I would return the favor you did me, María. I am who I am now, among other reasons, because for a while I was you, Justo Ramón."

"And I'm happy for that," María said, moved. "I did what I had to do. You don't owe me anything. You deserve all that you have—you're the one who did it, you alone."

"'Love and do what you will,'" Justo Ramón added. "We're followers of Augustine here, as you can see. You don't owe us anything. But if you don't want to feel selfish, maybe you should go back to the hotel and be with your family."

On the way down the stairs to the street, Leon was still asking himself if he had gone there to settle accounts with his past. The whole ride back to the hotel in the taxi, he didn't find the answer. Nor when he tried to distract himself, to think of anything to avoid suffering through a night of insomnia, nor the next day, in the company of his family, who were irritated at his unexplained absence the day before.

What bothered Donna most was all that empty time without a word from him. Now he was silent again, and she knew it would be a waste of her time to expect an explanation. At first, she had imagined Puerto Rico would be like Rome, and he would use the time away from home to confess something to her. Was there another secret from his past, or some crazy new project? But no, no confession had come, not even the night after his disappearance, when Jean opened the door well past midnight and crawled into the hotel bed in evasive silence.

"Everything OK, Jean?" Donna had whispered.

"Go to sleep. It's late, we'll talk tomorrow," Leon had said unconvincingly.

The next day, as though to appease everyone and make up all at once for time lost, Jean threw himself into making plans, not just the ones he had already promised, but other escapades they hadn't even discussed. Over breakfast in the hotel dining room, he tried to share his enthusiasm—before, he had always managed to. He kept saying how fortunate he was to have the family he had, and he joked with his children about how they had grown. In a few months, Jean-Georges would be eighteen; he still hadn't decided whether to go to college or look for a job like his father. Cécile, who'd just turned fifteen, wasn't a little girl anymore. She was turning into a beautiful young woman, and that made her father worry.

Throughout the day, Donna just nodded along and hid behind her sunglasses, never taking them off until they were back home in California. Only then did she stop feeling like covering her eyes.

"Why did we really go to Puerto Rico, Jean?"

Donna's voice was calm as she unpacked the suitcases and Jean undressed. The return trip on the plane had been rocky, and they had arrived home exhausted. The children were already asleep in their beds.

The weekend had been intense for the entire family. A disappointment for her. And a revelation for him. Another one that he didn't know how to share—or didn't want to share—with his wife.

"I already told you . . ."

He was a gifted liar. Once he'd internalized the version of a story that worked best for him, he could repeat it perfectly, never mixing up the details, and it was almost impossible to catch him in a contradiction.

His insistence wound up making his words seem, if not true, then at least plausible. His friends and acquaintances had long given up trying to pierce the veil of his obfuscations.

But Donna wasn't just a friend or an acquaintance.

"I know you better than that," she interrupted him. "Just tell me the truth. Why did you want to go there? You think after all this time together I don't know when you're hiding something?"

Donna knew her suspicions were justified. They were the fruit of countless disappointments and deceptions Jean had brought her through the years. He was on edge, and she could sense it.

"Did you find what you wanted, at least?"

Jean looked at her in silence, tried to evade that feeling of the four walls closing in on him.

For a long time, he hadn't truly been there. Whole years, in fact. And it dawned on him that now, at long last, Donna didn't want him around, either.

CHAPTER 16

Jean and Donna's marriage ended quietly in the autumn of 1976. It had lasted twenty-two years.

"There you have it, Emilio. Your grim predictions came true."

"I hate it for you. What are you going to do now?"

Jean removed a wine key from his pocket. He took his time removing the cork from a bottle of wine he had chosen especially for the dark occasion. He poured two glasses and raised his to deliver some inspired words. He had found an answer he hadn't wanted to hear in Puerto Rico.

"What I've always done, *mon ami*. Look ahead," Jean told his old friend.

Emilio didn't even toast.

True to his word, Jean looked ahead. And soon he found what he'd been looking for, right in front of him, at least for a time. Among the team of servers at the restaurant, there was a charming woman named Karen. A year after his divorce, he married her. Karen was good-looking, exuberant, and younger than him, with a daughter from a previous marriage. But when she began to act erratically and they diagnosed her with schizophrenia, that spelled the end of their relationship. Jean had never had much room in his life for the sufferings of others, and he wasn't going to put his projects on hold, even to help someone heal.

He had always bucked limitations; now wasn't the time to become a Justo Ramón trapped in the bed of new responsibilities. No, he wanted to remake himself, to become young again.

A little like La Scala, which was now crowded with new faces taking over for the stars and public figures of the past. This was the next generation of the fascinating, frenetic, corrupt world that bridged luxury, money, and power. The restaurant welcomed superstars and their pet eccentricities, politicians, athletes, unscrupulous millionaires, and boring rich socialites with ambitious hangers-on.

The changing times forced Jean to reconsider the business and diversify his offerings. He opened two new restaurants—La Scala Boutique and Au Petit Jean, both with front windows that opened onto the bustle of Beverly Drive. The decoration was a tribute to Mediterranean cuisine: empty crates of select brands of pasta, imported bottles of olive oil, packets of breadsticks, jars of olives, anchovies, peppers, artichokes. Bottles of Chianti hanging from the ceiling, and in strategic corners, magnums of Jean Leon, a brand that was starting to make its mark—not only at La Scala, but in places he had never dreamed of: the cellars of the biggest and most admired restaurants and hotels in the world, on the recommendation lists of prestigious wine critics and sommeliers, and in the homes of eminent figures in the world of wine.

Jean Leon even made it into the hands of an old companion, a fellow dreamer, who remembered it with fondness. On January 20, 1981, the streets of DC were frozen, but all of Washington was in its finest apparel to offer a warm welcome to Ronald Reagan as president of the United States. The president's inaugural banquet was catered by La Scala, but more importantly, Jean Leon's wine was there. *Dreaming is free.*

Was it Jimmy or Jean who had uttered those words? He no longer knew. What he was sure of was that Reagan had managed to predict the future that night—even if, sadly, his vision had only come true for two of them: *For you, a great wine; for Jimmy, a successful career. For both of you, a restaurant, and for me . . . heck, maybe I'll be president of the United States of America.* Reagan had raised his glass and said to Jean Leon, with a certain solemnity, *When we make our dreams come true, we'll toast our successes with your wine.*

It wouldn't be just any wine. The occasion demanded the very best from his winery, a wine that would serve to cement the brand's reputation: Jean Leon Cabernet Sauvignon Gran Reserva. That wine, produced at Château Leon in Torrelavit, his beloved winery in Penedès, the fruit of his efforts and sacrifices, would be known and recognized all over the world after that banquet. Professor Amerine had already predicted it. And so just as, long ago, the wines of Penedès had accompanied the feasts of imperial Rome, now Jean Leon and his wine were welcoming the new leader of the most powerful empire in the Western world: the fortieth president of the United States of America.

Seeing his wine served at the banquet for the incoming president of the United States catapulted Jean Leon's career. After the inauguration, Reagan even issued him a special license plate with the tag *JLEON* so that he could access any of the federal buildings in DC, including the White House, without problems.

Reagan wasn't the first president Jean Leon had served. The late John Fitzgerald Kennedy and Lyndon Baines Johnson, as well as Richard Nixon and Gerald Ford, had been his guests. But there was no doubt about it: this was a very special order. For five days, all the Hollywood stars and the rich oil magnates from out West would mingle in the bars, hotels, and inner chambers of DC with Republican politicians who'd come from all over the country to celebrate one of their own making it into the White House.

On the banks of the Potomac, the Kennedy Center hosted performances by Les Brown, Lou Rawls, Tony Bennett—and that was just the tip of the iceberg. At the Sheraton, Ray Charles, Patti Page, Wayne Newton, and the Mills Brothers would all be playing. Tommy Dorsey,

Glenn Miller, and Count Basie would trot out their repertory for the many parties that had been organized all over Washington.

Expectations ran so high that the president's inauguration was broadcast on live TV. The gala was produced, directed, and presented by someone who knew and commanded the scene like none other: Frank Sinatra. The president's table, set for eight, was in the center, the others arranged around it in circles.

At the rehearsal, Jean watched the master of ceremonies directing everything with his natural grace. Sinatra was at the top of his form. He would ascend to the stage where the orchestra was, then come back down, explaining to the lighting and sound technicians how to best cover each speech and performance. He was, no doubt about it—apologies to Johnny Carson—the best master of ceremonies of all time.

Organizing that event helped Sinatra regain the trust of the White House—this time, a Republican White House. In 1961, the actor and singer had overseen JFK's inaugural gala. He had been a committed Democrat, but after being cold-shouldered by Kennedy for his supposed mafia connections, Sinatra started leaning more to the right.

Reagan gave him the last nudge he needed when he intervened with the Nevada Gaming Commission on his behalf. After losing his gambling license in 1963 in the fallout from the Giancana affair, he was applying for a renewal to become the entertainment consultant for Caesars Palace. Reagan wrote a letter to the commission supporting Sinatra, whom he described as an upright and honorable person. When Reagan put in writing that the rumors about Sinatra were just that, and that there had never been any solid proof of mafia ties, he won Sinatra's support. And now Reagan was in Washington, and the new president had entrusted the Voice with organizing a very special party to celebrate his induction into the White House.

Jean remembered how Sinatra's magnetism had seduced him in his Villa Capri days. When they saw each other from across the room at the rehearsal, they gave each other a brief wave. They'd made peace a long time ago now, and everything was fine between them.

A huge swath of the Hollywood elite would file past hours later, dressed to the nines, as protocol demanded. From Charlton Heston to William Holden, Elizabeth Taylor, Burt Reynolds, Glenn Ford, Robert Stack, Patti Page, and Kirk Douglas. Jean regretted that Dick Powell, the man who had pulled strings to make it all possible, couldn't come watch Reagan take office, but a terrible cancer prevented him from being there.

Jean had lots of work to do that night, and he decided to leave off with the feelings and reminiscences, even though the music was giving him goose bumps. It wasn't just any old melody—for Reagan, it had a special meaning. The trumpets, trombones, french horns, and tuba gave the piece an imperial air: it was music to greet the arrival of a new president, and it encouraged the listener to join in. The entire audience stood.

The National Symphony Orchestra welcomed the president with a suite Erich Wolfgang Korngold had composed for the soundtrack to *Kings Row*, the film that had been Ronald Reagan's high point as an actor. Leon knew how moved the president must feel. He had no doubt that beneath Reagan's dapper tuxedo, he was shivering at the memory of a movie that would mark his entire career.

Leon saw Reagan take the hand of Nancy, who wore a white dress of needlepoint lace and satin with precious stones, one of her shoulders elegantly and suggestively uncovered. She wore matching white satin gloves that ran up her forearms to the elbows. Her shoes and handbag, the latter encrusted with jewels, gave her a regal appearance. To Leon, she looked like a queen, a Republican queen, and no one could take their eyes off her.

As the last bars of the music died out, the president and the First Lady reached their table. Before sitting down, they waved to the applauding attendees. Sinatra grabbed the reins, and the first dishes emerged from the kitchen under Jean Leon's supervision. Off in a discreet corner where he wouldn't bother the guests during that momentous occasion, he was surprised to find himself suddenly the center of attention.

"Today I raise a glass to toast the future of this country," Sinatra proclaimed. "And I want you all to know, you're doing it with an excellent wine. A wine made by my old friend Jean Leon, so let's give him a warm round of applause."

The public responded with a long ovation. Then, with his typical roguish smile, Sinatra couldn't help but add:

"By the way, Jean, I'll never forgive you for opening La Scala and competing with me! That's why I had to open Puccini, to stop you!"

The guests broke out into warm laughter. Leon laughed, too, and shook his head, marveling that despite all the years that had passed, Sinatra still hadn't gotten over the fact that Jean had been more successful in the high-end-restaurant world. It hadn't been a betrayal, and Jean knew Sinatra had forgiven him. Now the singer incited everyone to stand and raise their glasses.

"A glass of wine to celebrate the past, to enjoy the present, and to toast the future."

Because dreaming is free, and I still have a lot of dreams to make come true, Leon added to himself, convinced his story wasn't yet over.

EPILOGUE

The Port of Le Havre, France, January 1981

Life went on at La Scala and away from it, too.

After the presidential ball, Jean felt driven to face new challenges, find new motivations. Santa Monica, Hollywood, LA, the US were all becoming too small for him. Penedès and Barcelona weren't enough, either. He wanted to go further. But he was dogged by that feeling of incompleteness, of eternal dissatisfaction, and he knew that before he opened a new door, he would have to close others behind him.

There were six famous names that had marked him forever: James Dean, Frank Sinatra, Marilyn Monroe, John Fitzgerald Kennedy, Elizabeth Taylor, and Ronald Reagan. Four actors—well, five, counting Ronnie—and two presidents. Then there were Uncle Ramón, his cousin Julio, the Buenavida family. His two ex-wives, his children, and a winery with his name. Not to mention the Carrión family. But there was still one old, lingering debt, and the time had come to pay it.

He knew where to start looking. He had a name (and maybe even that was false), the memory of a tattoo, and a place. He went alone. It had been thirty-two years since that summer of 1949, and in that time, the port of Le Havre had been rebuilt. Jean walked over the promenade by the sea, with its views of leisure boats and merchant vessels. It was a beautiful, luminous stroll that led all the way to the loading docks. He repeated his inquiries tirelessly: to the stevedores young and old, to the maintenance staff, to anyone who seemed part of the ecosystem of the port.

All he needed was a hint, a little clue, a maybe. No luck. His life had been full of unexpected twists and turns, times when fate had smiled on him. Why couldn't it happen once more? It was just a matter of insisting, of persevering, of not giving up . . . of not complaining. And of being in the right place at the right time.

Leon was convinced he would find that man. Joe. The sailor who had helped him cross the Atlantic as a stowaway on the *Liberté*.

They told him to try at the Maison de la Mer, but it turned out to be closed. He left Quai de Southampton and walked down the surrounding streets. His steps took him to the Rue Georges Braque. He walked into La Taverne Paillette. He liked the traditional look of the outside, and the interior didn't disappoint him in the least.

Like a good restaurateur, the first things he took note of weren't the sights, but the scents, the feeling the place gave off. Here, you could breathe calmly. The decor gave him a feeling of trust, of comfort and peace. Then he regarded the other details: the order, the cleanliness, the people who would take care of him. The first impression, the one that counted, had satisfied him. His eyes grew moist. He remembered Donna and their conversation years ago, when La Scala was first opening, about what was most important for a restaurant to succeed. *You've got to take care of the details, the things people don't see,* she had said.

A tall, lanky waiter came to meet Jean with a smile, and invited him to sit at a table. Leon thanked him with a nod. The kid laid out the menu and the wine list and made a gesture that suggested he'd be back soon to take Jean's order. Jean took out his glasses and read the dishes and wines on offer. Seafood, local sausages with sauerkraut, escargot, salads. In the end, he decided on an old favorite, *moules au Roquefort*: mussels with blue cheese, parsley, and fried potatoes, a classic, but hard to find in America. Most of the customers were drinking beer—the place had its house brand—but he opted for a wine from Alsace, a Zind Humbrecht Riesling, not too dry, not too sweet, a perfect pairing for the sharpness of the Roquefort.

After the meal, when he was sipping his coffee, the waiter ventured a question.

"Excuse me, sir, you're not from here, are you?"

"No, I'm American."

"Ahhh, American. On vacation?"

"More or less. Actually, I'm looking for someone."

"Someone from here, from Le Havre?"

"I don't know. I don't think so." The waiter's face showed his confusion.

"Yeah, I know, it's strange." He smiled, realizing it was difficult to understand. "I came here on a hunch with nothing solid to back it up. But there's something that tells me this person may have stayed here."

"What makes you think that, monsieur?"

"Nothing," he replied. "Nothing at all. I don't have a clue. I know it's crazy, but I just thought I'd find him here."

"Oh, it's not a woman?"

"No," Leon replied with a smile. "No, no. A man," he clarified. "A sailor, someone who was very important to me."

"Ah, *bon*!" the kid replied, thinking he'd already asked too many questions. "Ask Mr. Taylor." He pointed toward the bar.

There, drinking a beer, seated at a barstool, was a man in a faded green military field jacket, bent over slightly, his cap pulled down low. Jean was shaken. He was a sailor, dark skinned, with piercing eyes. *It's unlikely, but it's not impossible.* His heart skipped a beat, and for a moment, he thought, *Could it be him?*

The man downed his drink, and as he placed the bottle on the bar in front of him, Jean caught his eye.

"Can I have a word with you?" Jean asked the man in a scratchy voice.

"As you wish," the man replied.

"Can I get you another? A beer, maybe? Would you join me?" Jean gestured to the empty seat at his table, looking Mr. Taylor over closely as the sailor raised the bill of his cap in agreement.

The man had a hard time getting down from the barstool. It took a few slow, heavy movements for him to drag himself from the bar to Jean Leon's table. The sailor touched his thigh and sighed deeply.

"This leg has been my perdition," he said, frowning with pain.

"What happened?" Jean asked.

"Let's say it's a keepsake from my years at sea."

Jean was unsettled. His nerves made him excited and impatient. The old sea wolf in front of him began to talk, telling him stories about other immigrants like Jean. He said that in his day, he had helped lots of young Italians and Spaniards make it to America. It wasn't for nothing that thousands dreamed of making it to the port of Le Havre to cross over to the Promised Land, to live their dreams of finding work and a place where they could have a future.

"I said to myself, who am I to wreck another person's dreams?" the sailor told him. He opened his arms, looking like an immense albatross beating its wings over the sea. "Life has its share of ups and downs, and it's hard to get through them. So I told myself I'd help those poor souls as much as I could. There were lots of sailors like me who wouldn't tell if they found a stowaway or two. We'd hide them and take care of them until they reached their destination."

He paused, as if sifting through his memories. "I used to always think about how, if I was in their shoes and the chips were down, I'd hope I could meet someone with a little humanity, who'd treat me like a person and not just some package you can throw overboard because . . ." He took a sip of the beer the waiter had left on the table. "Just think, that's what happened to some of the poor guys when they ran into crew members who didn't think like we did."

"They'd just throw them into the sea and not think twice about it?" Jean asked.

"Yeah, yeah, it was that bad. I saw it happen more than once, and there was nothing I could do," the sailor confessed. They sat there in silence.

Jean Leon thought how he would give anything to see if the man's forearm sported that tattoo: a ship surrounded by a thick rope, an eagle above, with outstretched wings, and below, an anchor with that phrase, forever etched in his memory, though at the time he hadn't understood the words. But with the man's turtleneck sweater and green field jacket, it was unlikely he'd get the chance.

Jean had had to flee his country, his family, against his will. He hadn't protested. He hadn't complained. He'd had to do it, there was no way around it. He'd had to go in search of the future, a dream that wouldn't have been possible for him if he'd stayed.

The sailor grunted and kept talking.

"I had a couple of partners who shared that same philosophy; we had a kind of unspoken deal, and we all took an oath. What makes a person strong is knowing how to keep a secret. If you can't keep a secret, you're lost. Especially on a boat."

When Jean heard those words, he couldn't help but ask, "Really?" Then, with a trembling voice, "You know something? All this . . ." He almost couldn't get the words out. "All this you're telling me is the same thing that sailor said to me. He knew how to keep a secret, like you, and he saved me."

Mr. Taylor laughed.

"I told you, those of us who felt that way . . ." He trailed off.

"Could I ask you a favor?" Jean's voice was full of excitement.

"Of course," the sailor answered with a surprised expression.

"Would you mind rolling up your sleeve?" He had to try and calm himself, because his heart was pounding out of his chest.

"As you wish." And as he began to do so, he warned Jean, "But I gotta tell you, what you're going to see ain't nothing pretty." Then he added, "Can I ask why?"

Jean, whose eyes were centered on that sleeve getting shorter and shorter under the sailor's hand, stayed silent, not listening, just holding his breath.

The rolled-up sleeve revealed a bare forearm, its skin aged and scarred. Jean's face showed his deep disappointment.

"I told you that you wouldn't like what you saw," the sailor continued. "It's from a fire we had on board years ago. I got bad burns on my arms and back. It reached all the way down into the cabins. It was a miracle we survived!" the man remembered.

That revelation brought the shine back to Jean Leon's eyes. If he'd had a tattoo there, the fire would have obliterated all trace of it.

"What do you care about my forearm anyway?" the sailor asked.

"I wanted to see if you had a tattoo . . . ," Leon admitted, slightly embarrassed. "The guy who helped me had one I've never forgotten."

"Ah, the tattoo!" the sailor repeated, smiling. "Yeah, I had one. Actually, we all did. It was our way of picking each other out."

"Excuse me?" Leon asked, perplexed.

"The tattoo, I mean. It was the symbol of the Brothers of the Sea. That's what I wanted to tell you, we felt we had a duty to help out people trying to get across, so we formed a kind of brotherhood. On almost every ship there were some of us, and our numbers increased every day. Since some people didn't see things our way, we needed a way to distinguish ourselves, and we ended up settling on some lines from a sailor-poet, Luther Ripley, who worked on the *Tiger*, a whaling ship, in the nineteenth century. It was perfect. *Growl you may, but go you must!* Every time we found a stowaway, those of us in the brotherhood would meet eyes and touch our arm where we had the tattoo. And that meant we had to act."

"So you were one of the Brothers of the Sea?"

"Yes, I was," the sailor replied firmly.

Just as he was about to ask the man's name, Mr. Taylor began to pull the conversation in other directions. Instead of pressing the matter further, Leon let him talk. There was no point in trying to figure out if the man in front of him was Joe, the man who thirty years before had made it possible for his dream to become reality. The man didn't want to go into it, and Jean respected that. Maybe Jean wasn't ready to know the truth about him, either.

Their chat stretched on over a few more beers and coffees, until Jean decided it was time to go. They took leave of each other with a handshake, and as Jean Leon walked out of the restaurant, he couldn't help but think that by tying up those loose ends, with all the coincidences that had come up in his conversation with Mr. Taylor, maybe he really had found Joe. *Why not? If there's one thing I've learned in all these years, it's that anything's possible.*

And as he whistled a melody from Sinatra that had popped into his head, "Me and My Shadow," he walked slowly back to his hotel. He identified with the lyrics to that song, which reflected solitude, individualism, and silent, constant work. In the end, it was him and his shadow, him and his circumstances. Alone, and sure of himself.

ABOUT THE AUTHOR

Photo © Author's Archive

Martí Gironell i Gamero is a journalist and writer born in Besalú in 1971. His debut work, *The Bridge of the Jews*, is the bestselling historical novel ever written by a Catalan author and has sold over one hundred thousand copies. He's written several novels set in different periods of Catalan history. He currently works at Catalan national television TV3 and writes for the newspaper *El Punt Avui*. He is considered a master of the popular historical novel, and his novels have brought renewed interest and fame to forgotten yet fascinating figures of Southern Europe's history.

ABOUT THE TRANSLATOR

Photo © Beatriz Leal Riesco

Adrian Nathan West is a literary translator and the author of *The Aesthetics of Degradation*. He is a frequent contributor to the *Times Literary Supplement* and the *Literary Review*; his work has also appeared in the *London Review of Books, Frieze*, the *New York Review of Books, McSweeney's*, and many other journals in print and online. His translations include Juan Benet's *Construction of the Tower of Babel*, Rainald Goetz's *Insane*, and Marianne Fritz's *The Weight of Things*.